I0566331

A Song in the Night

—— BASED ON A TRUE STORY ——
FELICIA LANDIE

A SONG IN THE NIGHT
Copyright © 2024 by Felicia Landie

Scripture quotations taken from the Holy Bible, King James Version, which is in the public domain.

Soft cover ISBN: 978-1-4866-2654-0
Hard cover ISBN: 978-1-4866-2655-7
eBook ISBN: 978-1-4866-2656-4

Word Alive Press
119 De Baets Street Winnipeg, MB R2J 3R9
www.wordalivepress.ca

WORD ALIVE
—P R E S S—

Cataloguing in Publication information can be obtained from Library and Archives Canada.

To Mark, my loving husband and friend.

Prologue

February 1908

A baby's shrill cry pierced the night air. Elsa blinked awake, shaking herself from sleep. She'd been dreaming of sailing with her husband. Sweet memories from their courting days often replayed in her dreams.

Pushing back the covers and making sure not to wake Jespar, she tiptoed across the cold floor and eyed the restless infant. The child had wriggled her arms free from the swaddle and held them up for her mother.

Elsa reached for the girl, nestled her on her shoulder, and moved towards the rocker. Back aching, she eased into her seat and put the baby to her breast. Motherhood was beauty, love, pain, and sorrow all wrapped up in one.

She knew the joy far outweighed the struggle, but would the nights ever get easier? She knew this baby would grow and one day sleep through the night, just like her older daughter had.

But Elsa wasn't sure she'd make it till then. She was so tired. Little Janet kept her on her feet throughout the day, and sweet Betsy awoke almost every hour at night. Was Elsa doing something wrong? Perhaps she wasn't producing enough milk. Perhaps the child was just too hungry. If only she were stronger. If only she had more to give. Jespar had offered to buy formula—it wasn't as if they couldn't afford it—but Elsa was unsure. She wanted to do it herself. She wanted to be capable.

As the baby ate lustily, the young mother heard crickets sing outside her window and the tall grandfather clock tick in the hall. Elsa prayed her own heart could find such a steady rhythm.

At last the child drifted off to sleep, and she tried to keep herself from doing the same.

As Elsa sat in the darkness, holding her precious girl close, she began to sing. She knew the baby didn't hear, and she hoped her husband wouldn't either. She'd never done this before, but tonight she felt desperate. It was as though her own heart needed soothing, and slowly she felt the Lord's peace wash over her. She didn't need to be stronger, for he was more than enough.

As she looked down at her darling child, a tear fell. She loved this baby so much that it hurt sometimes. But the love she felt for her children paled in comparison to God's love for her, and tonight she needed to remember that.

And so she sang. She sang to herself a lullaby.

Chapter One

July 1918

"Stop being scared, Betsy," her older sister said bossily. "I'm sure the preacher's boys are very nice."

Betsy didn't want to move, but her sister's grip was tight. It was a comfortably cool day in July. The sun was high and bright over the little town of Zeist, and a crowd had gathered outside the church. They still had ten minutes to spare before the service, and everyone was wearing their best Sunday clothes and best Sunday smiles, eager to meet the new minister and make a good impression.

Eight-year-old Janet Baer stood resolute and proud beside her timid younger sister. Forever watching out for her, whether asked to or not, Janet eyed the new family with curiosity, intent on making a new friend.

"We should go and make introductions," she declared, smiling in the newcomers' direction.

Staring at the boys across the churchyard, Betsy nudged closer to her sister. While the minister and his wife were busily engaged in conversation on the church steps, their two sons stood a stone's throw away by an old rosebush, talking to each other and curiously eyeing their surroundings.

"I'm sure they're very polite," her sister continued. "They're clergy after all! Maybe we'll show them the tree swing after service."

Tugging Betsy along, Janet finally approached the boys. The older one had wild blond curls and kept a firm hand on his younger brother, who fiddled with his buttons.

"Hi," Janet greeted the boys bravely. "My name is Janet Baer, and this is Betsy. Our dad is the head deacon. What are your names?"

"I'm Bram!" the younger boy said cheerfully.

"Hush up, poophead." The older one flicked his brother's brow. "I told you not to talk to anyone."

"Why ever not?" Janet asked, hands on her hips.

Betsy inched even closer to Janet.

"Cause we don't like church people," the boy retorted, kicking another pebble with his shoe.

Stunned, Janet fell silent.

Betsy was caught off-guard too, but she wasn't about to speak. She turned and looked at her sister, wondering how she'd handle things. She always handled things.

"Are… are you the minister's sons?" Janet asked, wondering if she'd gotten her facts wrong.

"Yeah." The boy crossed his arms. "But I hate it."

"Don't say that," Janet scolded him. "We're not supposed to hate anybody."

"I *don't* hate anybody," he replied. "I just wish my father was a soldier or a policeman. Then I wouldn't have to sit in church."

"You *have* to go to church," Janet replied. "Don't you know anything?"

"I wouldn't have to if I was a heathen." He smiled, anticipating a heated response. He then turned and looked at Betsy for the first time, giving her a little wink.

She blushed.

"Bram and me…" He draped a hand over his brother's shoulders. Bram seemed resigned to being outshone, and Betsy could relate. "We're gonna be soldiers."

Janet swallowed. "Don't you want to be a minister like your dad?"

"Heck no," he said, laughing.

Janet gasped and reached for her sister's hand. She thought it a very respectable profession.

The boy turned to Betsy. "What's your name, good-lookin'?"

Betsy reddened even more, but Janet was quick to come to her rescue. "Don't you ever call my sister that again!" She gripped Betsy's hand so tight that Betsy thought it'd fall off. "In fact, don't you ever talk to her at all."

Yanking her arm, Janet led them up the church steps. The service was about to commence.

"Come, Hank," the boys' mother called. "Bring your brother!"

Hank. So that was his name.

Janet led Betsy to the ladies' side of the sanctuary.

Mother wasn't at church that morning. She was expecting the new baby any day and the doctor had told her to rest. Betsy missed her, especially when Janet got overbearing. Betsy didn't mind Mother telling her what to do, and she'd never question Father's words, but when Janet pretended to be the third parent, it made Betsy's ears hot.

"Come on," Janet commanded.

Growing impatient, Betsy followed. It wasn't like she was the one who'd offended her sister, yet now she was getting her arm practically torn from its socket. But forever obedient to her sister's wishes, she sighed and sat down beside her.

Their brother Arend sat with their father and the other men across the room. She noticed the minister's sons taking their seats. Hank met her gaze and winked again. Betsy quickly looked away.

All fell silent as Reverend Vischer went to the pulpit for the first time. Betsy wished she didn't have to look at him. He looked so big and intimidating up there. Unsmiling, his voice sounded like a thunderbolt. It was loud, sudden, and made her tremble. Sometimes he would look right at her, and she felt as though he was peering into her soul.

"I'm not to hear a word from you," their father had reminded them that morning.

Betsy had promised to be good. Though it was her younger brother who most liked to goof around, she would nearly burst into tears when Father rebuked them.

The minister led the church in singing hymns. At least Betsy liked this part. The music was so beautiful, even though she couldn't read the words in the hymnal. When her mother was well enough to attend, she'd whisper her a line or two so she could sing along.

She turned and looked at Janet. Somehow her sister knew all the words, or at least she pretended like she did. Betsy watched in amazement. Janet always knew what to do and never got in trouble. The two of them would stand together with Janet looking straight ahead, almost unblinking. When the minister began to shout, Betsy would grab Janet's hand and squeeze it tight. Janet was never afraid, but Betsy often was.

The minister preached for a long time and Betsy tried to be good, but it seemed like hours passed and her stomach started to growl. It was so loud and she just knew everyone could hear it. Wrapping her arms around herself, she tried to ward off the noise. It didn't do any good.

"Hush!" Janet whispered, putting her finger to her mouth.

Little Claudia Van Hogan heard and giggled, and Mrs. Veenstra turned from the seat in front of them and shook her head vigorously. It seemed that everyone had heard.

Even the minister turned and looked at her. She didn't know what he was talking about, but it felt directed at her. He may have been talking about Elijah on the mountain or John the Baptist in the river, but all she heard was yelling and rebuke.

Janet jabbed her ribs. "Be quiet," she mouthed, as if Betsy could control any of this.

All of a sudden, from across the room, Betsy heard someone cough and then sneeze. Everyone turned. It was Hank Vischer himself.

The minister stopped midsentence, glaring at the boy. Hank had stolen any attention she'd been getting, and she breathed a sigh of relief.

But after the service, she saw his father take him by the collar and walk him around back.

"He must've been dreadfully sick," little Arend commented as they walked home.

"Or terribly disrespectful," Janet retorted.

Or really nice, Betsy silently added.

September 1927

"Do you wanna be my girlfriend, Betsy?" Bert asked.

From her swing, Betsy stared at the small teenage boy, dread rising up inside her. He'd pestered Isa Van Hogan relentlessly last year until she finally gave in and went on a date. But things had dissipated during the summer, and now Bert seemed intent on making another girl's life miserable until she obliged him. He'd cornered her when class was dismissed for lunch.

Janet had foreseen his intentions toward her younger sister on the first day of school, but Betsy had tried to ignore it. There was no ignoring it now.

"Why don't you like him, Betsy?" her friend Ada had asked. "He's rich, like you."

Betsy didn't like being called rich. Sure, her father was a shipbuilder. But she liked to think she didn't act rich. Her father was stern and didn't spend money frivolously. Mr. Van Aller, on the other hand, seemed to spoil his children rotten.

"Bert's got a thick skull," Janet had told her. "Some people think they know everything."

Betsy didn't know if she liked the boy or not. He wasn't especially good-looking or good-natured, and he picked on her a little too much.

She looked down at her shoes, her mind returning to the present. "I hardly know you, Bert."

"We've gone to school together for years." He took a step closer and touched the swing's chain below her hand. She instinctively pulled away. "We could go to the Sunday social together."

When he grinned, he showed a set of crooked yellow teeth. Betsy made up her mind that she didn't like him.

"No, Bert. I don't want to go," she replied, eyeing her friends over at a nearby bench. Why had she chosen to swing today? Why had she left the pack? The bear always went for the lone sheep. She stood and smoothed her dress, preparing for a quick exit.

"Do you like someone else then?" Bert asked, prolonging the conversation.

"No, no one," Betsy answered too quickly.

Bert stared at her in disbelief. "It's one of the minister's boys, isn't it?"

Betsy blushed.

"Which one is it, Betsy?"

"Neither, Bert. Don't be a pest."

"It better not be Hank. Rumor has it he's gonna drop out of school, and my father says he's a good-for-nothing pagan."

"Stop it!" Betsy replied, her own fervour catching her off-guard.

"It's true, Betsy. Hank Vischer's got nothing on me."

At least his teeth aren't crooked, she wanted to say. If only she could be as bold as Janet. If anyone had talked about her sister's friends that way, Janet would slap them good. But in truth, Janet thought as little of Hank Vischer as Bert did. For some reason, Betsy was the only one who saw any good in him.

She wanted to bolt. Tears brimmed in her eyes and she wasn't sure why. People said she was far too sensitive. Perhaps she hurt for Hank, perhaps she was offended by Bert's claims… either way, she wanted to run back to her friends.

Evading the boy, she headed in their direction, even as she heard Bert behind her: "Mark my words, Betsy. Hank won't amount to any-thing. He's…"

His words trailed off… for she was running like the wind.

May 1933

Blond curls swayed freely from side to side as the little girl bobbed on ahead of her. "I want ice cream!" she pleaded.

"We'll see." Betsy smiled, trying to keep up with her charge.

She and little Femke had walked nearly two blocks to the playground, another four to the pond, and now they were making their way downtown to get a treat. The girl had dirty elbows, a bruised knee, and a few scratch-es. Betsy had tried to wash her off in the pond and suggested they go home for a bit, but Femke wouldn't have it. She was so like Betsy's sister, Janet: stubborn. But the girl was also irresistible. Betsy had worked for Femke's parents for a year now, and this little dear had stolen her heart.

"We'll just get something small," she said, catching up to the girl. "We don't want to spoil your supper."

"When will Mama be home?"

"After you're in bed, Femke."

"I want to see her now," she whined.

Betsy pulled her into her arms.

"Mama…" Femke mumbled, nestling herself into the crook of her neck. The girl's chubby thumb quickly slipped in her mouth and her rosy cheeks went to work.

Betsy's heart ached. "I know you miss your mama," she whispered.

I miss mine too, she wanted to add. It was the reason Betsy had taken this job. Her own mother had been ill for so long. Even when Betsy was little, her mother's cancer had wreaked havoc, both on her body and in their home. When her children needed her, only doctors and nurses had been allowed near. Betsy would've given anything to have been by her side.

At least being a nanny, Betsy could offer the care she wished she'd had from her mother. At least she could be there for children like herself who missed such motherly affection as she had.

But there was one difference between her sorrow and Femke's. Betsy's mother hadn't been able to care for her, because she'd been sick. Femke's mother chose not to care for her, because she was too busy. The girl's family was among some of the wealthiest people in Zeist. They lived in a grand house and employed a large staff to clean, cook, and, for the last few years, care for their three-year-old daughter.

"Why do you wear your hair like that?" Femke was never at a loss for questions. Her little fingers reached up to touch Betsy's braid. Yanking it, then getting caught in the strands, Femke giggled.

Summoning her patience, Betsy untangled it from the child's grasp. "It's supposed to keep it out of the way," she said with a smile. "So I can keep up with you."

Tapping the girl's nose, she winked. Femke giggled heartily.

Delicious smells greeted them as they entered the ice cream shoppe. The owner not only sold cold treats, but he made all his baking from scratch. Femke wriggled from her arms and dashed towards the counter, cutting in front of a few patrons.

"I want strawberry!" she squealed.

Betsy sped after her and smiled nervously at their fellow customers. "Sorry," she stammered, taking Femke's hand.

"Hey, little lady, I'll be with you in a minute," came a friendly voice from behind the counter.

Betsy smiled. It was Bram Vischer, the minister's younger son. They'd been in the same grade, but after graduation she'd seen him only sporadically. He and his brother had gotten jobs in Utrecht, which had taken them away for quite some time. She would've hardly recognized him but for his charming grin.

When they got to the front of the line, Bram leaned on the counter and winked at Femke.

"Hi Bram." Betsy smiled, subconsciously adjusting her braid. Did he think she looked older? It had been a few years since high school.

"Good to see you, Betsy!" He grinned. "How're things?"

"Good," she answered quickly. "Could we get a scoop of strawberry?"

"In a cone!" Femke added.

"You bet!" Bram laughed, opened the freezer, and grabbed a cold metal spoon.

Fumbling with her purse, Betsy tried to make conversation. "You back living with your parents?"

Bram nodded, handing the girl her treat. "We are. There was nothing really keeping us in Utrecht, and Mother begged us to come home for the summer. Who knows what we'll do after that?"

"We?"

"Hank too, though a little more grudgingly as you can imagine." Bram laughed. "You look swell! Seeing anyone lately?"

Betsy blushed. She had never been on a real date and Janet said she was too shy for her own good. She'd heard through the grapevine that Bert had moved away, and no one else had really taken an interest in her. Her friends told her she needed to put herself "out there" more, whatever that meant. But no matter how hard she tried or how much she wanted a boyfriend, she couldn't seem to get one.

She rummaged in her purse. "I'm not dating anyone."

At this, Femke yanked on her skirt, a pink moustache above her lips. "Are we done yet?"

Betsy retrieved her payment and turned to go.

Bram stopped her. "Care to go to the spring dance tomorrow night?"

Betsy swallowed. Part of her wanted to find an excuse. She had to help Janet at home. She had to care for Femke. She had a garden to weed.

"I'd love to," she heard herself say.

Bram smiled approvingly and Femke was off. Betsy spun around and spotted the girl skipping towards the door.

"I must go!" Betsy started then turned back towards the handsome clerk. Was he going to pick her up?

"Meet you there?" he asked.

She nodded. Then, turning on her heel, she fled after her ward.

As she ran, her mind also raced. What would Janet say about all this? Would she be happy? A date *was* a date, and she had never had one. But Bram Vischer? Forever in his brother's shadow, Janet had never paid him much mind. Neither had Betsy. His brother, on the other hand, had irritated Janet to no end, and now rumour was that Hank didn't even go to church. Betsy wondered why. She wondered where he'd gotten a job or if *he* was seeing anyone. She wondered what he looked like now.

She blushed.

Passing beneath the towering pines and turning the corner, she wondered whether Bram was now her boyfriend. How did one know? If the first date went well, were they considered a couple? Would he ask her to marry him one day?

"Oh, Betsy, how you dream," she whispered to herself as she and Femke came in sight of the mansion.

Femke's parents employed a full-time gardener to keep the grounds- and everything was in full bloom. The tulips and crocuses had boldly ushered in spring. Betsy smiled. They were her favourite flowers, and when she got married one day she wanted to carry them in her bouquet.

Janet would roll her eyes if she knew Betsy's thoughts.

But Betsy couldn't help it. Bram was a nice guy. He always had been, and maybe she'd be his wife one day.

But as she carried Femke inside and started getting her ready for her nap, she had but one question on her mind: did Hank have a date for tomorrow?

Chapter Two

"I say, your hair is much too lovely to wear in a braid every day," Janet remarked as she combed Betsy's mane. "I've got the perfect hairdo for tonight. You're going to love it. But my goodness! Won't you sit still?"

Betsy squirmed in her chair, trying to do as she was told. Their room was in utter disarray. More than a dozen dresses, blouses, and skirts covered the wood plank floor, and hair bows, ribbons, and hats graced the nearby bed.

As Betsy had feared, Janet was unsure about her sister's date. She tilted her head. "What even *is* his job?"

Betsy shrugged, "Ice-cream, I guess."

Janet rolled her eyes. "Well, perhaps he's still wanting to be a minister," her sister put forth hopefully. "Wasn't that what he was planning to do after graduation?"

Nodding, Betsy winced. Janet was ruthless with the tangles.

"What's his brother up to?" Her sister reached for a spray bottle. "I'm guessing *not* attending seminary." Sarcasm dripped from each word.

"I don't know!" Betsy surprised them both with the quick reply. Her cheeks warmed. "Bram said they're here helping with renovations for a while. Hank was always good at tinkering."

"Tinkering in other people's business," Janet fumed, poking Betsy with a hairpin.

Wincing again, Betsy recalled Janet's run-ins with Hank. Growing up, he'd always gotten a reaction out of her, and so she'd taken the brunt of a few jokes. Janet, in return, had brutally pestered and scolded him.

"Hank has got nothing going for him." Janet was stuck on the subject. "No religion that we know of and a bad reputation."

"He was always nice to me," Betsy interjected, surprised by her own conviction.

And he's very good-looking, she wanted to add.

While most people had disliked Hank, only her brother Arend had taken her side. The two boys had worked the same first job at a grocery store. Arend said they'd have good chats about world events.

Arend had got on well with him, but Arend got on with everybody.

Sticking in the last pin, Janet smiled approvingly. "Well, let's just be thankful you're not going out with Hank Vischer. His brother seems a lot more agreeable."

Absentmindedly, Betsy nodded. Her stomach was a ball of nerves. She sat, playing with her hands, trying to be still, unable to stop fidgeting. Wrapping her arms around her stomach, Betsy tried to take a deep breath, but a tear ran down her cheek instead.

"Oh, Betsy, you're far too sensitive," Janet admonished. "Why on earth are you crying?"

"I don't know." Betsy sighed. She was happy but anxious, thrilled and terrified all at the same time. "I've never been on a date before. What will it be like?"

"You're asking the wrong person," Janet retorted.

Betsy shrugged. Her sister had hardly had any more experience than she had with such things.

"Put your tears away and pull yourself together." Janet squeezed her shoulder. "It's about time you were off."

Betsy wished it were that easy.

Grabbing the hairspray, Janet applied a generous mist. Betsy coughed from the smell, resisting the urge to wipe her thickly powdered face.

"How do I look?" she squeaked, afraid of the answer.

"It'll do."

Betsy just sighed. Her sister *did* have a way with words.

Quietly descending the steps, careful not to wake her mother who was resting in another room, Betsy caught sight of her father, brother, and young sister in the entry. Their house boasted expensive draperies, rugs, and wall hangings, things father had insisted on purchasing and of which Betsy was sometimes embarrassed. Though Jespar Baer was wise with his money, he also liked to show it off every once in a while.

"Ready to go?" her brother Arend asked.

Betsy nodded. Since she didn't like driving at night, he and his wife Angela were to drive her and her younger sister Hannie. Janet had flat-out refused to attend, or else she would've taken the wheel.

Brow furrowed, Jespar Baer turned to face his middle daughter. But when he spoke, it was to his son. "Keep an eye on your sisters now. Bring them home at a reasonable hour, you hear?"

"Yes, sir." Arend smiled, pulling on his coat.

Eyes still on Betsy, Jespar then addressed his youngest daughter. "No antics, Hannie. The Baers are respected in this town and I'd like to keep it that way."

Though she seemed offended, Hannie nodded. "Yes, sir."

Having gotten her baby down for the night, Angela appeared. The girls got their coats and headed for the door.

Jespar saw them out with one final word, this time to Betsy herself. "This is only a dance, Betsy. Though Bram is pursuing an education, which is far more than I can say for his brother, he has nothing but a smile to recommend him. I want better for you."

"I'll try to remember," Betsy stammered.

♪♫♪

The town hall was bustling. Lanterns hung from the rafters and young men and women mingled amongst themselves. The band was tuning up and prize-winning cakes and cookies decorated the buffet table.

Though Femke's parents loved to host parties, Betsy rarely attended. She was often busy watching Femke, and she'd always turned down her friends when they'd pushed her to attend. Incredibly shy, Betsy had always found an excuse.

Tonight she'd found her courage. She'd said yes to Bram and made it all the way to the hall without begging Arend to turn the car around, though she'd wanted to.

She stood beside Arend and Angela, Hannie having long abandoned them for her friends. Embarrassed to hold them up but fearing being alone, Betsy frantically searched the room for her date.

Arend smiled. "See your fella?"

Betsy shook her head.

"He's got to be here somewhere," Angela encouraged. "Arend, why don't you dance with Betsy first?"

"And leave you?" Arend seemed torn.

"I'll go chat with Mrs. Gerbrandy. I see her by the window."

Though forever kind, Arend looked reluctant.

Betsy shook her head. "It's okay, Angela. I'm sure Bram is around here somewhere."

"Well, he better not leave you too long…" Angela put her hands on her hips. "Or another chap might just snatch you up."

Betsy tried to smile, but her lip trembled as she watched them go. Suddenly the room felt very large indeed. The smells of coffee and baked goods, which had previously made her mouth water, now seemed repulsive. The floor squeaked as people moved about, getting into dancing positions, and Betsy felt terribly conspicuous.

Where in the world was Bram? The music was starting and her date was nowhere to be found. She wished she hadn't come. If only she'd made an excuse, she could be comfortably at home with Janet, reading a book or baking cookies. She'd even clean a cupboard or two if it meant she could escape these prying eyes.

Throat parched, Betsy moved towards the drink table. How long could she take filling her glass? Maybe she could go to the ladies' room and reapply her lipstick, or perhaps she'd simply find a closet in which to spend the evening.

As she neared the punch bowl, she heard a familiar voice call her name. "Betsy!"

Turning, she spotted her friend Ada.

"What are you doing here?" the girl asked, laughing. She didn't mean to be rude, but all Betsy's friends knew she didn't attend these gatherings if she could help it.

"Hi." Betsy smiled, relaxing a little. She was thankful to see a familiar face. "I came with Arend…"

"That's new!" Ada exclaimed, her boyfriend appearing by her side. "Do you have a dance partner? I'm sure Pieter could find you someone—"

"No!" Betsy cut her off. "I mean… I have a date."

"You *do*?" Ada could not hide her amazement.

Betsy's hands felt clammy. "Yes."

"Who? You said you came with Arend."

Betsy wished she'd come with Bram. At least she'd know where in the world he was. "Bram," she felt compelled to say.

"Bram Vischer?" Ada grinned. "I actually just saw him by the buffet table. Is he getting you something to eat?"

Speechless, Betsy searched the food line. Sure enough, there was Bram, talking with Femke's parents. For a moment, she felt relieved, but it soon gave way to more anxiety. Why hadn't he found her sooner, and what would she say when he did? Should she go over there, or was she just supposed to wait for him to find her?

Thankfully, she did catch his eye, and he quickly excused himself from his conversation and made his way over to Betsy.

"Good evening!" he said amiably. "Sorry I didn't find you sooner. There's so many people I need to catch up with… so many old friends!" He turned to Pieter and Ada. "Like you two! How are you?"

Betsy's cheeks burned. Was she selfish for wanting his attention? She didn't exactly have experience with this sort of thing.

The three chatted briefly, before Bram turned back to her. "Can I get you some punch, Betsy?"

She nodded and he was off. Pieter and Ada went to dance, once again leaving Betsy alone. She watched Bram fill two glasses before immediately getting swept up in another conversation.

Betsy contemplated making a quick exit. Perhaps she could convince Arend to drive her home.

Scanning the room for her brother, she was suddenly aware of someone again by her side. Bram had returned with the punch.

But as she turned, she realized it was very much not Bram. Standing beside her was none other than Bram's older brother.

"Good evening," Hank said with a smile.

While her heart had been racing, it now launched into somersaults. "Hi."

She swallowed and tried to study the man through her tears. Betsy tried to blink them away.

"Is everything okay?" he asked.

Betsy was immediately aware they were being watched. The older men and women who hadn't hit the dance floor now glanced at them sideways and exchanged a few whispers. Like his brother, Hank hadn't been around for a few years. But unlike Bram, he had a bit of a colourful reputation.

"Yes," Betsy lied. "I mean… I was just about to leave."

"Leave?"

Tears subsiding, Betsy blushed. In some ways, Hank resembled his brother, but in others they were completely different. They both had sky-blue eyes and white-blond hair, but Hank's features seemed more intense. He was also taller and broader…

Betsy dropped her gaze, embarrassed he might read her thoughts.

"If you must go…" Hank sounded disappointed. "…would you at least give me one dance?"

Betsy did love dancing, but she wondered what Bram would think. What would everyone think? But for some reason she didn't care.

"Yes," she replied.

Taking her hand, he led her into the centre of the room and they joined in seamlessly.

Growing up, Betsy and her siblings would have pretend dances, and when well enough Mother would teach them some steps. Betsy was glad they came back to her now.

Hank effortlessly moved her about and she couldn't help but smile. His hands felt calloused and he was obviously very strong, yet he moved her gently.

Betsy tried in vain to focus on her steps.

"Sorry," she said, stepping on his toes.

He winked. "Never mind."

The song seemed to end too soon and Hank led her to the window to get some fresh air.

"You're lovely, Miss Baer."

Betsy gasped. Her old anxieties returned and her stomach began to churn. What should she say? Suddenly she felt incredibly awkward and shy.

Hank noticed her discomfort. "Everything all right?"

"Yes," she said. "I'm just shy, I guess. Mother says I have 'nervous stomach.'"

"I think I know what'll help." Reaching into his pocket, he pulled out the tiniest radio she'd ever seen. "Do you like music, Miss Baer? Or should I call you Betsy, like I used to?"

Betsy nodded to both questions. "Where'd you get that?"

"I found it in a trash bin and fixed it up." He tapped the front proudly. "Good as new."

Betsy marvelled. "I'm very impressed."

"I hoped you would be." Handing her the machine, he tilted his head. "You can have this. Maybe music will make you feel better."

Feeling awkward, Betsy didn't know whether she should accept such a gift.

She shook her head. "I can't take this."

She began recalling all the rumours she'd heard. Hank had quit going to church, jumped from job to job, and was at odds with his father. He was a reckless sort, but for some reason she had always been taken with him. Janet had never understood, and frankly she hadn't either.

He smiled. "Please take it."

Betsy couldn't resist smiling too.

"Take what?" Bram appeared beside them.

Betsy silently slipped the radio into her purse.

Not waiting for a response, Bram turned to Betsy. "Sorry, I just got talking again. Here's your punch. Would you like to dance?"

"You shouldn't have left your date waiting so long, little brother," Hank said, turning to him.

Betsy swallowed.

"I *am* sorry," Bram apologized again. Taking Betsy's arm, he grinned. "Care to dance?"

Reluctantly, Betsy nodded. Why did she feel so torn? Hadn't she been waiting for Bram this whole time? Hadn't she been anticipating this moment ever since he had asked her out?

But now, as she walked into the crowd, hand on his arm, she could only think of one person—a dashing radio repairman.

Chapter Three

Betsy had never been inside the little grey house, though she'd walked past it more times than she could count on her way to church and school. Located just behind the church, the modest structure had certainly seen better days. The white picket fence had chipped paint and a squeaky gate that didn't quite latch. A few shutters had blown off in the wind and the roof needed to be replaced. She knew people looked to her father to organize such things; he wasn't only the head deacon but also the wealthiest man in the congregation and always very generous. Betsy had never quite figured out whether he did it out of his own freewill or her mother pushed him to it. Either way, the church was reliant on Jespar's financial contributions. Betsy was sure her father hadn't meant to let the parsonage get so rundown, but with Mother's illness and his company's booming success, he'd been a little preoccupied lately.

Having walked across the park and up First Street, Betsy arrived just in time. Heart fluttering, she ascended the front steps and knocked on the door. Bram had invited her for dinner, for he'd said he wanted her to meet his parents. When she'd told Janet this, her sister had laughed. Hadn't they known the Vischers since they were girls?

Not like this, she had wanted to say.

But what was *this*? She didn't have any clue. Bram had invited her to the spring dance and nearly forgotten about her half the night. Janet had told her not to get her hopes up, that he probably wasn't interested, but to her surprise Bram called on her the next day—and the day after that. In fact, they'd been spending time together for a few months.

"Would you like to go on a walk?" he'd asked her the other day.

They'd walked to town and gotten sundaes, though he'd never offered to pay.

He'd smiled as they parted and said, "You're a great friend, Betsy!"

Betsy had sighed. After all that time, were they still only friends?

But now this. Meeting his parents. What did it all mean? She was excited that Bram might like her. He was attractive, kind, and the pastor's son! What more could she ask for? She hoped he would make his intentions clear, and she hoped he intended to date her.

The door opened and Mrs. Vischer appeared. The woman seemed to look older every time Betsy saw her. She never seemed very sure of herself, and to Betsy she always looked sad.

"Hello Betsy," the lady said with a smile, taking her by surprise.

Was that the first time Betsy had ever seen her do that? However, the expression quickly faded as the woman ushered her inside.

The room was too warm and Betsy eagerly slipped from her coat. "Thank you for having me for supper."

The woman attempted another smile as she hung up the jacket. "Bram speaks very highly of you," she mused, moving them toward the kitchen.

Betsy suddenly felt even warmer. There were no pictures on the walls nor curtains on the windows. A stack of large books covered a nearby shelf and a few old chairs served as the sitting room adjoining the kitchen.

A booming voice made her jump: "I see our guest has arrived!"

She turned and saw Reverend Vischer emerge from the other room and take his place at the table. Betsy had often jumped at his words, but it was usually as he spoke from the pulpit. He too had never looked happier.

After what seemed like an eternity, Bram appeared. Ironically, he seemed the least animated of them all. He said hi, sat down quickly, and motioned her to do the same.

Betsy wondered whether Hank would be joining them as well. Turning to Mrs. Vischer, she asked after him but quickly regretted doing so.

"Hank is otherwise engaged this evening," Reverend Vischer answered for his wife, a note of finality in his tone. "He will not be joining us for supper."

Betsy nodded, surprised by her disappointment.

After Reverend Vischer said the blessing, Mrs. Vischer retrieved the pot of soup from the stove.

"Couldn't we have made something better for our guest?" Reverend Vischer laughed, almost mockingly.

Mrs. Vischer's face reddened.

Embarrassed for the woman, Betsy shook her head. "I love soup. My mother makes the same one, I think."

"Mrs. Baer cooks?" Reverend Vischer seemed surprised. "I would've thought she kept a maid to do that."

Betsy swallowed. There were a lot of things people assumed about them. Being wealthy sometimes felt like a curse rather than a blessing.

"My father doesn't like to spend money on things we don't need," she said. "My mother loves to cook... I mean, she did."

Betsy didn't want to talk about that. Her mother had recently been too sick to do anything.

There was silence for a moment.

"Do *you* cook, Betsy?" Mrs. Vischer asked, ladling out the warm liquid.

Betsy took her bowl gratefully. She wished she didn't have to answer so many questions. Usually Janet did the talking, and Betsy suddenly missed her.

"I like to bake," she said, faltering. "Though I'm afraid I'm not very good at it."

Turning to Bram, Betsy wished he'd say something. Why was he so quiet? He'd been so animated at the ice cream shoppe. Even at the dance, he'd been more talkative. Why was he so distracted? Was she making a good impression, if that was what this was all about?

Finally, Bram did speak, but it was only to his father. "I've started my seminary application."

Betsy dropped her head. That meant he'd be leaving.

"You should have started weeks ago," came his father's quick reply.

All went silent except the clinking of their spoons.

Mrs. Vischer turned to Betsy. "Bram is hoping to attend seminary in the fall."

Betsy plastered on a grin. "That's wonderful."

"Only it costs a fortune," the minister said, shaking his head.

"Bram is hoping to be a minister in Zeist one day." Mrs. Vischer smiled hopefully. She seemed to anticipate having her son around more.

Betsy nodded. She wondered what it would be like to be a minister's wife. If she were, she hoped she wouldn't be half so miserable as this lady seemed.

"Bram tells us you're a nanny," Reverend Vischer said. He seemed to be sizing her up. She wondered whether she was acceptable.

"Yes," she answered bravely.

"Do you like children?" Mrs. Vischer eyed her son as she spoke.

Blushing, Betsy perceived the implication. "I do. They're lovely."

Reverend Vischer took a generous gulp of water, then set his glass down with a thud. "I'm surprised you need to work, what with your father's large income."

Feeling defensive, Betsy spoke without thinking. "My father wants us to be independent, to be able to take care of ourselves if we need to. He always says, 'Handouts don't create successful people.' You'll never find him giving out his money on a whim."

As soon as the words left her mouth, Betsy realized what she'd actually communicated.

Though Betsy and Mrs. Vischer still had soup left in their bowls, Reverend Vischer pushed away from the table, pretending not to notice. "You must excuse me, Miss Baer. I'm afraid I must do some organizing in my study."

Bram quickly shot up from his chair. "Do you need help, Father?"

"Don't be ridiculous." The man waved aside the offer, seeming suddenly indifferent to everyone and everything.

As the man made his way down the hall, Bram called after him. "I'll work on my seminary application tomorrow."

"You should look for a better-paying job too," his father muttered, entering his study and slamming the door.

Betsy jumped again.

Bram stood looking after him for a moment, and Betsy almost felt sorry for him. Though she was frustrated by his lack of attention, she sympathized with the young man. She'd felt frustrated by Reverend Vischer's questions and hadn't wanted to make things harder for this family. Things seemed tense enough.

While her own father could be harsh, she never doubted his love for her. Her mother was physically weak, but she radiated joy. Reverend Vischer, on the other hand, was coldness itself, and his wife always looked like she'd been crying. It was no wonder Hank rebelled. Betsy couldn't imagine growing up in such a home.

"Bram, why don't you show Betsy your writings?" Mrs. Vischer asked.

"You write?" inquired Betsy, turning to him.

"Not much." Bram looked defeated. "Just a few essays for my application."

Betsy gulped. She didn't know whether she'd understand a word, but she agreed to look them over.

Mrs. Vischer got to cleaning up, and the two sat down on the couch. An awkward silence ensued as the evening wore on. Arend had promised to pick her up at nine and she tried not to keep glancing at the time.

Suddenly, Betsy heard voices outside. They both turned as the front door flew open.

"I've never seen anything so ridiculous!" someone guffawed.

Before Betsy even knew what was happening, Reverend Vischer appeared from his study and Mrs. Vischer from the kitchen. Betsy turned to Bram, and he gave her a look that reminded her of a wounded puppy dog. What on earth was happening?

Straining to see what all the commotion was about, Betsy rose to her feet, catching sight of a tall young man in a brown fedora.

Hank.

Sander Dorenkamp and her brother Arend were with him, and the three were laughing about something. Betsy felt the hair on her arms and neck stand up on end. What in the world were they doing, and why were they being so obnoxious?

Suddenly, her head began to spin. Were they drunk?

"What is the meaning of this?" Reverend Vischer bellowed.

Hank stopped talking and looked the man straight in the eyes, smiling. "What do you mean, Father? Can't boys have a little fun?"

Chuckling, Hank slapped Sander on the back, while Sander stood smiling nervously. Arend was quiet.

"Have you been drinking?" Mrs. Vischer gasped.

"Just a few drinks, Mother," Hank said with a grin. "Don't tell me there's anything wrong with that."

"What a disgrace!" Mrs. Vischer now turned to Betsy, embarrassment written on every feature. Letting out what sounded like a wail, she disappeared into the other room.

Bram stayed frozen on the couch and Reverend Vischer went into a rage.

"You test my patience, Henry," he stormed, taking his older son by the collar. "When will you ever learn? Are you trying to ruin your life?"

Despite his slight intoxication, Hank grew serious. "You're doing a fine job at that, Father."

Reverend Vischer clenched his fists and Betsy wondered whether they'd come flying. But instead the man gathered enough composure to turn around and face her. Betsy swallowed.

"I think your visit is more than over," he muttered. Then, still facing her, he addressed her brother. "Take everyone home now, Arend. All of you must go, and I hope you'll keep the details of this evening to yourselves. More than a few reputations are on the line."

"Yes, Reverend Vischer." Arend nodded, eyeing Betsy so as not to waste a moment.

Betsy couldn't move quickly enough. Grabbing her coat, she was about to follow the boys out when Hank caught her eye.

"You're looking lovely tonight, Miss Baer." Hank smiled and winked his perfectly blue eyes.

Smiling back, Betsy lingered beside him. He was so tall and his arms looked strong. It'd been fun dancing with him the other night, moving about the room, her hand in his.

"Come, Betsy!" Arend called.

Reluctantly, she followed.

Sander took the front seat, as they'd drop him off first. But when she and her brother were alone and almost home, Betsy had to speak. Though Arend was a year younger, he had always looked out for her as an older brother would.

"What a terrible night!" Her words spewed out uncontrollably. "Oh, Arend. It was all just awful."

Her brother nodded. "Yeah, Reverend Vischer can be merciless."

"Is Hank really as bad as everyone says?" It was perhaps the first time she'd ever asked the question. Perhaps everyone was right about him. Perhaps he was a no-good heathen, despite his lovely eyes.

"I like him," Arend replied calmly.

"No one else does," she muttered.

Arend chuckled. "He isn't exactly well-liked in this town, but he's not a villain, Betsy. In fact, he's my good friend."

"Why would you be friends with someone like that?"

"Why wouldn't I?"

"People will start thinking you're just like him."

He laughed. "No, they wouldn't."

Betsy laughed too. Arend had the cleanest reputation of anyone she knew. He was forever the peacemaker, forever the confidant.

Betsy was quiet for the rest of the drive home. In truth, she liked Hank Vischer, really liked him. But would it ever work?

Reading her thoughts, Arend smiled again. "If you ever go for Hank, Betsy, you might have your work cut out for you. Father will need some convincing."

She smiled back. "Janet will too."

Chapter Four

September 1933

B etsy liked the smell of the hardware store. It was a mix of fresh lum-
ber and paint, and though she didn't like talking to strangers, Betsy
loved surveying the shelves.

It had been a week since her visit with the Vischers, and she hadn't
stopped thinking about it. More specifically, she hadn't stopped thinking about Hank. He'd always been good-looking, but he'd very much
grown up—and like Father's good wine, his appearance seemed to get
better with age.

As for Bram, he'd called on her once more, but it was obvious he'd
lost interest, and she didn't expect another date. Perhaps he'd find a new
wealthy young woman to pay his seminary fees. Betsy didn't mind. She
only wondered whether she'd have another excuse to see his brother.

Having been commissioned by Janet to get a new set of pruning
shears, Betsy made her way to the gardening corner, but she stopped
midcourse. Standing just a few feet away was none other than Hank
Vischer himself.

Noticing her as well, Hank turned from his basket of screws and
nails and nodded. "It was wonderful seeing you at the spring dance."

Knowing she was probably blushing, Betsy nodded, surprised that
he didn't mention their run-in at his parents' house. Perhaps he wanted
to forget the whole incident. She certainly did.

"I'd love to see you again." Hank grinned, a hopeful look in his sky-
blue eyes. "Can I take you to the cinema on Friday?"

Too stunned to think, Betsy mumbled something. Hank seemed pleased and said a few more words. Again, Betsy answered, but for the life of her she didn't know what came out!

Pleased again, Hank winked. "Till then!"

With that, he waved and sauntered away.

In a daze, Betsy purchased the shears and raced home. Racking her brain, she tried to remember what she'd told him. Had she agreed? He had been so friendly and thoughtful, and Betsy believed she had never seen someone so handsome. He liked her, that was obvious, and she loved to be liked.

But had she agreed to the movie? What movie had it been?

Seven o'clock on Friday. The time rang a bell. She was to meet him outside the cinema at seven o'clock.

She raced up the front steps of her home and headed inside. The smell of fresh pie greeted her, but she was too preoccupied to stop. Hurrying up the staircase, she hoped to avoid anyone in the hall. She had to think!

"Betsy, come see my new dress!" her younger sister Hannie beckoned, coming out of her own room.

At that moment, Betsy wished she were as headstrong as Janet, but she couldn't resist her young sister. No one ever could, and so Hannie was spoiled rotten.

"It's lovely," she murmured, hardly able to ascertain the colour.

Thankfully, Hannie was too self-absorbed to notice her distraction. Compliment received, her sister waltzed back to her bedroom and Betsy fled to the one she shared with Janet.

Closing the heavy door, Betsy set her shopping bag on the bed and ran to the mirror. Her hair was in disarray and she had a few too many freckles on her nose. Sighing, she grabbed her hairbrush.

Suddenly, the door opened and Janet appeared. "Did you get the pruning shears?" she asked.

Nodding, Betsy pointed to the bed. Janet mustn't know, but how would Betsy keep such a secret? Janet knew everything. She could look right through her and always had an opinion about what she saw.

Her sister picked up the bag and opened it. "Oh, not those ones," she said with a sigh. "Those ones are useless."

Betsy barely heard her.

"I'll just go myself," Janet decided, returning the bag's contents. She turned to face Betsy straight on, hands on hips. "I'm surprised you haven't graced the kitchen yet. I'm making apple pie. Mother said I may, since we're having guests over tonight."

"Who're we having?" Betsy asked absentmindedly, beginning to brush her strands.

Coming towards her, Janet took the brush and began to work, catching every tangle, making Betsy wince.

"I'm surprised you don't remember." Her sister laughed. "The Beckers? Their daughter, Renske, was in your grade? I seem to remember you were very excited to see her again."

Betsy had forgotten, and her sister looked suspicious.

"What's going on, Betsy? You seem like you're in another world."

Betsy hoped she'd be in Hank's world for a good long time. Trying to hide her secret, she smiled. "I'm probably just tired. Town was busy."

"Uh-huh." Janet raised an eyebrow. "Come to think of it, you've been distracted all week. Are you and Bram going out again?"

"No."

"You don't seem disappointed."

Betsy shrugged. "I guess it's just not meant to be."

"How mature of you to say." Her sister's words dripped sarcasm.

A moment later, Janet turned to go. "I'll head to town now. Be back before supper." Snatching the bag, she opened the door. "I'll take the pie out before I leave. Don't worry. I won't ask you, as you'll probably forget…"

Betsy hardly knew she'd gone.

It was Friday night. Betsy had helped Janet clean all day, and just before supper she read a few psalms to her mother. Elsa Baer had been bedridden for almost a year now and Betsy took every opportunity to be with her.

While she preferred reading novels, her mother had asked for Scripture today. Betsy obeyed but hardly remembered what she read. After finishing, she kissed her mother's forehead and headed downstairs to eat. If she was to meet Hank at seven, there was no time to lose.

She told Jespar that she was going to Ada's for the evening, and he nodded his approval.

"Ask her father to drive you home at nine," he instructed. Jespar Baer never let his daughters walk home in the dark, and he did not approve of late curfews.

Supper done, Betsy hurried upstairs to change. Hair pinned, make-up on, and sweater buttoned, she headed out. But just as she reached the front door, Janet appeared.

"I'll walk you out," she declared and grabbed Betsy's hand.

Betsy cringed as her sister tugged her along. Closing the door behind them, Janet looked her straight in the eye. Betsy wanted to run. She felt like a mouse caught in a trap, and she feared she'd been discovered.

"What's all this about?" Betsy asked, trying to feign ignorance.

"You better tell *me* exactly what it's about," Janet hissed.

Betsy took a step back, nearly falling off the porch as she did. "What do you mean?"

"You're not going to Ada's, are you? Are you seeing someone? It's written all over your face."

Betsy swallowed. If she told Janet who she was seeing, her sister would forbid her to leave the house again. As far as Janet was concerned, as far as most people were concerned, Hank Vischer was not a good catch. Being reckless, having a bad reputation, and believing in no religion to speak of, he was a bad influence, and yet Betsy liked him. She wanted to know him and she was flattered that he seemed interested. A tear escaped her.

Softening, Janet put her hand on her shoulder and sighed. "Oh dear."

Janet did care for her. Betsy knew that. It was why she was so protective, yet Betsy was often hurt by Janet's mother-bear ferocity.

"I won't tell anyone." Janet took her hand. "I'm just looking out for you."

"It's Hank," Betsy mumbled.

As quickly as it'd left, the fire returned to Janet's eyes. "Hank Vischer? I forbid it!"

"He's nice, Janet. He asked me to the cinema."

"A gentleman wouldn't ask you to sneak around."

"Well… he didn't exactly ask that—"

"Of all people! Hank Vischer!"

"Keep your voice down," Betsy urged. "I really do like him, Janet."

Stunned to silence, Janet was thoughtful.

"He gave me a little radio and asked me to dance and was so kind and—"

"Father will never approve."

Betsy nodded.

"Hank Vischer is a rebellious choice."

Betsy dropped her head.

"But… I suppose I can't stop you."

Betsy was flabbergasted. "Janet…"

"Let me finish. I can't stop you. But I will say this: no more sneaking. If Hank Vischer is going to try and win you, and win Father, he better do it right. He better pull up his bootstraps and be a man. He should date you properly and ask for Father's blessing."

Fearful, Betsy nodded. "And what about your blessing?"

"I'll think about it."

Now it was Betsy's turn to be speechless.

♪♫♪

Hank's jaw was tense. Standing together in her backyard as the evening sun went down, Betsy eyed him with curiosity. He'd talked to her father and asked if they could date, but how had it gone?

"He wants me to work at his company for a year," Hank muttered, shoving his large hands in his pockets.

"But did he say yes?" she stammered. Could she really be Hank Vischer's girlfriend? It seemed too wonderful to be true.

Hank threw up his hands. "One year, Betsy!"

"Is that really so bad? It would be a steady job, and maybe he'll let you stay on after that."

"Stay on?" Hank fumed. "Why would I want to work at his company? I like fixing radios. I'm good at it, and I want to make it my business. Why would I up and go build ships?"

Betsy loved Hank's free spirit, but in some ways it scared her. She knew her father wasn't being unreasonable, but she didn't want to further anger Hank by saying so.

"Would you do it for me?" she asked, surprised by her own forwardness.

Immediately softening, Hank took her hand. "I would do anything for you."

Other than when they danced, it was the first time their hands had touched. Betsy's heart leapt and she quickly scanned the windows to see where Janet was hiding. When she turned back to Hank, she saw him leaning in for a kiss. She darted away and ran for the door.

Before going inside, she turned and grinned. "See you at the cinema!"

September 1934

It had been one year—one year of picnics in the park, bike riding, and afternoon drives. They had bravely gone to family functions and Hank had been supportive as her mother's health worsened. Betsy often worried about her, but every time they were together Hank tried to bring a smile to her face. They'd dreamed of their future together and Hank had kept his word to work at Jespar's company.

Now that one year was up, Betsy anticipated what was next.

"I've been looking at properties to buy," Hank told her one night. They had ridden their bicycles to the nearby pond and found a place to sit to watch the paddle boats.

She smiled, unable to hide her excitement. "Oh?"

"I also asked your father's blessing to marry you." His words spilled out.

Betsy gasped, but Hank took her hand. Forever confident, or at least pretending to be, Hank touched her cheek. "There, I've said it. What do you think?"

"What did my father say?"

"What do *you* say?" He was teasing her, but Betsy's stomach was a ball of nerves.

Hearing a bird overhead, Betsy lingered, studying him. She loved Hank's adventurous spirit, and she thought he looked so handsome in the fading summer's light. The fire in his eyes burned brightly, and Betsy hoped he'd never lose that.

She loved his passion, and yet a hundred questions rose up inside her. Was she ready to be a wife? Did she have what it took? And what about Hank? Though he was wonderful, he had a wild streak. Could she handle that?

He didn't go to church and hadn't in a long time. But was that a problem? It wasn't like God was a big part of her life either. Sure, she'd always gone to church like she felt she was supposed to, but would that change when she got married? And what would her mother say if she was well enough to communicate? Unlike almost everyone else, Elsa Baer had never spoken badly of Hank. She'd understood that they were dating, and she'd told Betsy he was a nice boy. But she'd also prayed. Betsy had sometimes overheard her doing so, praying for Hank and praying for her.

Betsy's stomach started to hurt. It'd been too long since she'd heard her mother's voice.

"I love you, Hank," she finally whispered, a tear slipping through.

Seeming to read her thoughts, Hank pulled her close and stroked her hair.

When she looked at him again, she saw that he was mulling something over. "Your father wants me to work another year at the company. It was again his stipulation."

Betsy nodded.

"It seems everyone is trying to stop me from pursuing my dream. Radio is my passion, but I know people think I'm crazy."

"I don't think so." Betsy touched his scratchy cheek.

A fishing boat paddled by and Betsy seemed to detect the smell of a woodfire. The sun had almost set and they best be getting home, but just before they left Hank drew near and kissed her. For a fleeting moment, all her worries melted away.

Chapter Five

December 1934

Betsy's mother had gotten so pale these last years. Her creamy skin had grown ghostly, and the body that'd carried and embraced four children was now skin and bones. The doctors had said she didn't have long, but Betsy had only begun to believe the truth: her mother was going to die.

She carried a tray up the stairs, laden with weak tea and thin oatmeal. The house felt cold and dark, like it was holding its breath. The doctors had given up trying to feed the woman, yet Betsy hoped she could eat. She'd always been the sweetheart of the family and easily able to get her way. She hoped her persuasive powers even held sway over a dying body.

Reaching the top of the oak staircase, she tiptoed towards her parents' room. The door was closed and the room within dark. Out of habit, she knocked on the door, then inched it open. Her mother's almost lifeless body lay still on the bed, multiple quilts stacked on top. Janet had tried to no avail to get her warm, ripping quilts off every bed in the house and stacking them like pancakes.

The woman's eyes were closed, and with the curtains drawn Betsy could barely make out her face. She moved towards the bed, the air stale and sour. She and Janet had worked tirelessly to keep things clean, but the smell of illness and approaching death lingered.

Placing her warm hand on her mother's, she felt nothing but ice. Catching a glimpse of her mother's face, she barely recognized it.

"Mother?" she whispered, a knot forming in her throat.

Her mother's once thick, honeycomb hair had all but disappeared, though a few dry whisps held on for dear life. Like Betsy, they seemed to cling to hope.

Betsy set the tray down on the nightstand and ran her fingers over her mother's brow. She drew close and kissed her cheek, willing life into the woman's cold frame. Lifting her mother's head, she tried to put the teacup to her lips. Her mother didn't respond. Betsy then dipped two fingers into the lukewarm drink and touched her mouth. Her mother's eyes slowly moved, the first signs of life.

"Mother?" she whispered again.

Her mother blinked slowly and studied her. Somewhere in the recesses of her memory, Betsy saw recognition, a love that had burned brightly and inspired everything the lady put her hand to. Now that love was only a faint glimmer, a flame that was almost extinguished.

"I'm scared, Mother," Betsy breathed. "They say you're going to die. I don't believe it, but I'm scared… what if they're right? I can't imagine life without you."

A lump formed in her throat and she couldn't speak anymore.

Her mother continued to hold her gaze.

But Betsy wanted to be held for real. She wanted to be wrapped up like she used to be and have all her worries rocked away. She wanted her mother to speak life into her fearful heart.

"How could God take you away from us?" she spoke again. "I feel so alone."

The woman ever so gently squeezed her hand, and Betsy could almost see her lips trying to move. Was she trying to say something? She leaned in close, straining to hear. Her mother tried to form words, but no sound came out.

Finally, she heard her mother's whisper. "You're never alone," she breathed.

Betsy wiped her tears, finding solace in her mother's voice yet fighting her words. She knew her mother spoke of God, but Betsy couldn't feel God like she could feel her mother's cold hand in hers, and she couldn't see him either.

Her mother was her world, and God felt like a vague idea. His presence was not a comfort, when her mother's life was slipping away.

That very night, Elsa did slip away… into the presence of her Savior.

♪♫♪

"Are you ready?" Hank touched her elbow.

Betsy would never be ready, but she was dressed, had braided her hair, and shrugged on her coat—if that's what he meant.

She nodded and the two headed out to the waiting car. Father, Arend, and Arend's family would ride in the first car. Hank, Betsy, and her sisters would ride in the second. The funeral was set for ten o'clock. They'd planned the service and invited many, yet all the details seemed a blur. Betsy's heart felt cold as a stone.

Hank took her hand and instinctively rubbed her engagement ring with his thumb. In just a month, she would be Hank's wife. Though she was excited, her joy now seemed overshadowed by grief.

Hank and Betsy climbed into the waiting car while her sisters got in the back.

"Are you all right?" her fiancé asked.

She didn't know how to answer.

January 1935

Their wedding day arrived. Her insides still ached, but she was happy. Hank Vischer would be her husband and she felt lucky.

The two smiled and laughed and made their vows. Janet was her bridesmaid and Bram the best man. They ate cake and people threw rice. Then, as the snow fell, they made their way to their new home.

Before they even changed out of their wedding clothes, Betsy lay down on the tiny bed they would now share, a knot forming in her stomach. She wanted to wish the pain away and be happy like she should be, yet her mother's seat had been empty today.

Hank lay down beside her and wrapped his arms around her waist. His warm breath kissed her neck.

"My angel," he whispered and began to sing a love song. Slowly the melody began to soothe her. The darkness lifted, if even for a moment. Music had a way of doing that. Hank had a way of doing that.

September 1935

Betsy stood at their kitchen window, basking in the warm sunshine as she worked. Eight months had passed and she loved being a wife. There had been a lot to learn at the beginning, cooking every day and managing a home for oneself. Sometimes she missed her family and the comfort of their presence. She'd call Janet to ask how to cook or wash something, and Janet would sigh, scold her for not knowing, but then seem pleased to offer her advice.

Their little house was everything she could've asked for. Hank had bought it with cash shortly before their wedding. They had a bright kitchen with a window overlooking the yard. A sturdy oak table sat in the dining room, something Hank had built before the wedding. Betsy knew it'd be big enough for lots of children—she hoped at least four. Their bedroom was just off the main room, right where it should be. Betsy remembered how Janet used to wish to sleep in the attic when they were young, saying it'd be quiet and cozy. Betsy had always thought attics spooky and preferred to sleep on solid ground.

She'd covered hers and Hank's bed with store-bought linens they'd received as a wedding gift, and she'd hung pretty blue curtains on the windows. She washed her laundry on the back step and dried it on the line. When it got cold, they warmed the place with a tiny stove, and at night the walls creaked in the wind.

Wanting a place to work, Hank was converting the old shed out back into a shop. But tinkering would have to do for now; though he dreamed of having his own repair shop one day, he'd bowed to her father's wishes and was working another year at the company.

Betsy now stood in her tiny kitchen, apron on, a pan of cookies in hand. Taking a deep breath, she looked around, thankful. It wasn't the grand house she was used to, for she'd grown up in luxury. But it was home.

Now it would be shared with a new little person. Betsy put her hand to her belly. She'd suspected as much for a while. After missing her last cycle, she'd felt nauseous like never before. She'd been tired, irritable, and suffered a few headaches, but she hadn't yet told anyone.

Janet was coming for coffee today and Betsy hoped she wouldn't spill the beans, at least not before she'd told Hank. Though she was miserable at keeping secrets, she wanted to wait to be sure. Her mother had miscarried several children and she didn't want to disappoint him if the worst happened.

Thankfully Hank hadn't discovered it yet, but Janet? She would notice. Her sister had the eyes of a hawk and could read Betsy like a book.

A knock interrupted her thoughts.

Betsy set the pan of cookies down and slipped off her apron. Moving towards the door, she opened it and met her eldest sister on the porch.

"Coffee smells delicious!" Janet grinned, never bothering with formalities.

As she entered, Betsy couldn't help but notice her sister's strong back and defined features. She was a proud woman who'd never cared much about her looks. She could've been beautiful if she'd only tried, but Janet had always been more concerned about living her life than fretting in front of the mirror. Betsy, on the other hand, had been a little too concerned about such things.

"Let me take your hat and sweater," Betsy offered, hanging both on a nearby peg.

The two moved towards the big oak table, where she'd set out their coffee cups. Like their dispositions, Janet preferred her beverage strong and plain, while Betsy was a cream and sugar girl.

"Don't tell Hank or he'll get a big head," her sister laughed. "But this table is quite the beauty. I admire it every time I come over." Janet sat down and ran her hand over the smooth finish.

"I am blessed," Betsy replied.

It hadn't just saved them money; the homemade table was much more meaningful. Her father had scoffed when he'd heard Hank was building it. Though a shipbuilder himself, Jespar had seen that his children always had store-bought everything.

"Is Hank still fixing radios?" Janet took a sip of her drink.

"Yes, he spends hours in the shop. I sometimes bring his supper out to him, when he forgets to come inside."

Janet eyed Betsy's abdomen with a knowing look. "He'll have to make enough for three pretty soon."

Betsy gasped. "How did you know?"

"You could never keep a secret from me, little sister."

"I haven't told Hank yet. I'm afraid he'll be worried."

Janet nodded. "I guess you'll both have to be brave."

Betsy was quiet for a moment. "Mother lost a few babies."

"And we lost Mother, but that doesn't mean we need to stop living."

Betsy swallowed. "How can you be so strong, Janet? Do you ever feel afraid?"

"Being afraid is a waste of time, little sister. Don't make a fuss over me." She pointed to Betsy's belly. "You've got a little one to think about now."

Chapter Six

October 1935

She still hadn't told him. It'd been a month since her sister's discovery, and two months since she'd found out for herself. Still she couldn't work up the nerve to tell her husband.

Hank had been overwhelmed these past weeks. Work at her father's company was far from pleasant. The wages were low and Jespar Baer wasn't a patient man. Though Hank worked hard, her father never seemed satisfied.

At least it's steady work, she told herself, which was more than she could say for his repair business.

Hank spent his evenings in the shop. It seemed to be how he coped. People had started bringing him furniture and gadgets to repair, and Betsy was proud of him for that. On more than one occasion, Hank had brought up quitting the ship company to officially start a repair shop. Betsy had tried to seem pleased, but fear lodged inside of her. There was no way he'd make enough to support a growing family. They were hardly making enough to live on as it was. Oh, he made sure they had the necessities. They always had enough for bread, milk, and a little meat. She'd grown a few vegetables that year and she looked forward to planting even more next spring. She tried to be thrifty with what little they had, giving up putting sugar and cream in her coffee, as plain was cheaper. She'd also quit baking so much. Hank didn't especially love sweets, and she just kept a few on hand for visitors.

But each month, despite all her attempts to save, they barely broke even.

Today was Saturday and Hank had the day off. He'd been working in his shop all morning and it was nearing lunchtime. Pulling on a coat, Betsy ladled some soup into a bowl, grabbed a spoon, and headed out back. Leaves crunched beneath her feet. A slight chill ran up her spine and she could almost taste the apples waiting to be picked from a nearby tree. Sounds of hammering caught her ears.

Upon opening the shop door, she laid eyes on her husband. Hank Vischer still took her breath away. His tall frame and broad shoulders were bent over a wooden object and a blond wisp of hair fell across his forehead. Not hearing her come in, he continued working intently.

She set down his bowl and moved towards him, careful not to step on woodchips, scraps of metal, and a handful of screws. She cleared her throat from the dust and her husband looked up, smiling.

"What're you building?" she asked, sliding her hands around his strong waist.

Hank leaned down and kissed her, his clothes smelling of sawdust.

"Has anyone told you, you look like an angel?"

Betsy blushed. It was what he always called her. It was her name. While she grew impatient with her sensitive heart, Hank adored her and treasured her innocence.

"You still haven't answered my question." Betsy laughed, playing with his shirt collar. "What're you working on?"

Hank kissed her one more time, seeming to avoid the question. "Well, I was going to wait till it was finished. But I see you've caught me."

Overwhelmed with curiosity, Betsy crouched down to inspect his project. As she did, she gasped.

Running her hand along the smooth wooden box and soft scalloped edges, she whispered, "A cradle."

How had he known? Had it been that obvious?

She stood to her feet again and met his gaze. "You're more perceptive than I thought."

"I wish I could say that was true," Hank said with a chuckle. "Actually Janet told me."

"She never could keep a secret." Then, worried, she asked, "Are you okay with it all?"

"Why wouldn't I be?" Hank asked with a furrowed brow.

"You've been so anxious about work lately, and I know things have been tight—"

"—and you're used to much more." Notes of both kindness and frustration seasoned his tone.

For a moment all they could hear was the old shed's windowpane rattling in the wind.

"That's not what I was going to say," she whispered. "I just thought that with how hard work has been and your talk about opening a business—"

"—I can take care of us, Betsy."

His voice rose in volume. He wasn't angry, but Betsy knew she'd touched a wound. People had questioned his capabilities all his life. His father had wanted him to be a minister, and her father wanted him to be wealthy. Hank just wanted to be free.

Taking his hands, she whispered, "You care for me so well."

Her husband sighed. "I'm sorry, my love. I didn't mean to get upset. You're right that it does weigh on me. You gave up a lot when you married me, and your father made sure I knew as much when I asked for your hand. I've tried to be content at his company... I've tried to make it work..." He dropped his gaze, contemplating his next words carefully. Looking up again, he smiled. "And I *will* make it work. I'll stay on at the company and work hard to provide."

"But your dream..."

He moved closer and put his finger to her lips. "*You're* my dream."

Betsy cupped his face with her hands.

Hank smiled and kissed her. "Do I smell soup?"

He laughed, yet Betsy could still see the sadness in his eyes.

April 1936

Armed with seedlings she'd started weeks ago, Betsy headed out to her designated plot. Hank had tilled it well the day before, and she'd drawn up a map to guide her. Squinting from the glaring sun, Betsy examined her rough sketch and began to mark off her rows with sticks. Asparagus and onions would grow at the front. She'd put the peppers behind them, and in a few months she'd plant beans and cucumbers in the other section. She'd lined the perimeter with tulip bulbs and the lovely flowers were almost in full bloom. She liked the reds and yellows best. They reminded her of her mother's garden when she was a girl, and the memory made her throat tighten.

Betsy would garden as long as her back would allow. Baby Vischer was expected in just over a month, and Betsy's growing belly proved it. Between the kicks, aches, and extra weight, she had very little energy to spare. Arend's wife Angela, who had herself birthed two children, said that Betsy carried quite large. Betsy wondered if the child would be as tall as Hank someday. While the thought made her smile, she prayed the baby wouldn't be too big. Childbirth sounded painful at the best of times, and Betsy was neither large nor strong. The pregnancy itself had been a challenge thus far.

"You've got to stay active," Janet would tell her.

The two went on walks almost every day. Betsy missed being able to bike, but such activity was far too strenuous now. Even simple things like cleaning and cooking were getting to be difficult.

Plunging her hands into the soft earth, Betsy worked back the soil to form little holes. She set the first seedling in place and covered the roots with dirt. Patting it gently, she moved onto the next.

She'd barely finished the first row when her back began to talk. A strong ache worked its way up her spine and she felt breathless. Sitting upright, she wiped her brow with the back of her dirty hand. How would she ever be able to finish?

She felt frustrated with herself. Other women did this all the time, didn't they? Angela had planted a huge garden every year while still keeping four little ones in tow. Why was Betsy always so weak? She hated feeling incapable. She hated her anxieties and aching back. Oh why couldn't she be stronger?

A noise broke into her thoughts. Straightening, she looked about, trying to place the sound. It was music—the soft notes of a piano drifting over the fence from the house next door. It was lovely and peaceful. Listening, she tried to determine the tune, for it seemed familiar.

As the music progressed, the melody grew louder and more distinct. The lyrics came to her and she couldn't help singing along. Lyrics from her childhood, a hymn she'd heard in church.

> Fear not, I am with thee, oh, be not dismayed,
> For I am thy God, and will still give thee aid;
> I'll strengthen thee, help thee, and cause thee to stand,
> Upheld by My gracious, omnipotent hand.

The pianist continued, repeating lines and adding their own flare. More lyrics came to mind and Betsy sang along.

> The soul that on Jesus doth lean for repose,
> I will not, I will not, desert to his foes;
> That soul, though all hell should endeavor to shake,
> I'll never, no never, no never forsake.[1]

The words penetrated her heart, sinking deep into her soul: *"Fear not. Be not dismayed. I'll strengthen thee, help thee, cause thee to stand. I will uphold thee. I will never forsake thee."* They were promises.

Betsy had heard the song before, yet she'd never really paid attention to it. But now, as she pressed her hand against her swollen belly, on the cusp of motherhood with new joys and challenges, she thought of her own mother. Though Mrs. Baer had been a woman of few words, the words she had spoken were forever etched in Betsy's heart. Her words could've been taken from this very song. They were truths on which to stand. *"God will help you. God will strengthen you."* And on her deathbed,

---

[1] John Rippon, "How Firm a Foundation," 1787.

she'd used what little strength she had to remind her daughter, *"You're never alone."*

Betsy hadn't believed it at the time, and she still struggled to do so. God always seemed far away and hard to please. She never felt good enough or strong enough, and she was sure God must be disappointed in her. Perhaps if she could be as good as Janet or as pious as Reverend Vischer, she'd feel peace.

Or maybe, if she just didn't go to church like her husband, she'd feel less burdened.

It seemed everyone was looking for peace in a different way, but her mother was perhaps the only person she'd ever known who was truly at rest. Her mother had shown her a different way. She'd not only loved God but seemed convinced that he also loved her.

The music began to fade and Betsy wondered who'd been playing so beautifully. There was only one old man living in the next house over, and he'd just moved in the other day.

Betsy hadn't thought much of it. But now her curiosity was piqued. If he'd been the one playing, she had to know. Where had he acquired his skill in the first place, and most importantly, did he really believe the lyrics to such a song?

"I think I'll bring him some cookies," Betsy decided. They had a dozen saved in their icebox, carefully stored for guests. She'd wrapped them in paper and hidden them away—a hard thing to do when you're eight months pregnant and have a sweet tooth.

But such a performance mandated some *spritskoeken*. She would plate them, eat some lunch, and then head on next door.

♪♩♪

She knocked hesitantly on the door, waiting for any sound of life. Eyeing her plate of *spritskoeken*, she sighed. There was one less than she'd planned, thanks to her lack of self-control.

Hearing footsteps inside, she instinctively moved back. The door opened and a white-headed fellow appeared. Hunched over with a leathery face, he eyed Betsy as if thinking he should recognize her.

"You a relative?" he asked, scratching his head.

"No, I live next door." She held out her plate. "I heard your piano music this morning and wanted to thank you for such a beautiful performance."

The man eyed her curiously, not taking the cookies. He tilted his head and put his hand to his ear. "You need to speak up, young lady. My hearing isn't what it used to be."

Betsy wondered if she'd made a mistake. How could a frail old man play such music? "I live next door," she spoke louder this time. "I heard your piano music. It was beautiful."

"Ah… you love piano music too? Smart young lady."

"Do you play other hymns?" she asked.

"The whole book. That's what my mother taught me from." He tilted his head again. "Where'd you say you lived?"

"Next door." Betsy pointed. "My husband is Hank Vischer. I'm Betsy."

"Ah. Diederik." He first pointed to himself. "Care to see the beauty?" He then pointed to the room behind him.

Betsy smiled. "I'd love to."

Betsy followed the old gentleman inside, through a tiny dark entry into an equally small sitting room. Two or three dining chairs sat around the perimeter, surrounding a grand piano.

She grinned. The instrument took up nearly every nook and cranny, and her host seemed pleased as punch with the setup. He ran his hand over the smooth black finish and looked up at her proudly.

"My mother left me this." Growing serious, he added, "Playing has got me through… many, many hard times."

"Indeed," she said with a nod.

For the first time, he seemed to notice her plate of cookies and her belly. "Let me get those. I'll have Eliana fix us some coffee. Please take a chair. You must be tired in your condition. I know all about pregnant women. My wife had a baby, you know. God rest her soul."

Betsy sat down, wondering if the man lived with his daughter or had a maid.

A young woman appeared and took the plate. Her hair and eyes were dark and Betsy wondered about her name.

The man pulled a chair near her. "Do you play the piano?" he asked.

Betsy dropped her head. "I wish I did. I guess I never had the patience for it."

"I learned when I was a boy. Did I tell you my mother taught me straight from the hymnal?"

The two were quiet for a moment, then suddenly Diederik looked up, an idea springing to mind. "Would you like to learn?" he asked as the young woman appeared with the coffee. "I've taught Eliana many songs... haven't I?"

The young woman grinned. "Yes. Mr. Vanderhoof has taught me many things."

Betsy's eyes widened. Perhaps one day she *would* learn.

Chapter Seven

May 1936

Sitting on her bed, Betsy clenched Janet's hand. The contractions were growing stronger and more prolonged. They felt like cramps, and they were so painful. When they started, she couldn't focus on anything but getting to the other side. They'd come on slowly the night before, but now they were only minutes apart. Her whole body would seize up and, though she tried desperately, she couldn't grasp a full breath.

"Nothing to worry about, little sister." Janet wiped her brow. "Women have been doing this since the beginning of time."

And dying from it, Betsy wanted to add.

Janet never gave in to fear, and she always knew what to do, which is why Betsy didn't want anyone else by her side. Perhaps her sister could be brave enough for both of them.

The midwife, Mina, had come an hour ago and quickly sent Hank to the shop. It wasn't the way of things to have men in a birthing room— that's what their bedroom was called today.

Hank had kissed her and been hesitant to leave, and she'd tried to put him at ease. But he'd seen right through her, for they were both afraid.

Betsy looked around, trying to steady herself before the next contraction. The pretty blue curtains on the window, the vase of crocuses on the sill, a tiny radio Hank had fixed up the previous winter—it was home. It was where they'd usher in this new life, where they'd raise their child. Were they ready? She felt too weak to push, much less be a mother. Closing her eyes, she did what she knew her mother would do.

God, I don't have the strength. Help me.

Another contraction. Her body seized, and this one seemed too overwhelming to bear.

Mina examined the progress. "It's time to push, Betsy," she said, smiling.

Betsy didn't know whether to smile back. Was everything all right? Was it supposed to hurt this much? She tried to breathe. She tried to gather any bit of strength she had left. She tried to imagine what this baby would be like. Who would they become? Was it a boy or a girl? Would they have Hank's white-blond waves or her honeycomb locks? Would they be tall and broad like their father or small like their mother?

Janet wiped her brow and tightened her grip. "You can do this, sister," she encouraged.

No, I can't, she wanted to say. *Jesus, sustain me.*

Suddenly she heard music trailing through the open window. She looked up and Janet turned to investigate.

"I think your neighbour is spurring you on," her sister said. "Hank must've put him up to it."

Betsy smiled wearily, listening again to the old hymn. *Fear not, I am with thee.* God was there. He would answer her prayer.

On the next contraction, she pushed with all her might—once, twice, three times. As the pain bore down, something strange rose up. Peace.

Within moments, it was over. A resounding cry pierced the morning air and her baby was in her arms. Though her legs quivered, Betsy laughed. The baby too was shaking, and she held him close to her breast. It was a boy, and she couldn't take her eyes off him.

"Well done, sister!"

"Shall I get your husband?" Mina offered.

Betsy just nodded. Mesmerized, she studied every feature, unable to stop smiling. He was perfect—a little tuft of honeycomb hair like hers, sky-blue eyes like Hank's. His cries subsided; sleep soon overtook him and Betsy planted a kiss on his milky skin.

Hank appeared by her side, his strong arm gently around her. She stole a look at her husband, but she had no words. Happiness overwhelmed her heart.

Hank gazed at their son in wonder, and today Betsy saw something different in his eyes. Something had changed. While they often danced with glee or warmed with compassion or steadied hers in strength, today they marvelled in wonder. He was like a little boy in a toy shop, and yet something shifted again as she handed him the bundle. He looked like a father, gentle and protective.

"I don't deserve this." Her husband's voice cracked.

Betsy took his hand.

"What will we name him?" her husband asked.

She'd had many ideas, even compiled a list of possibilities, but now one name rose above the rest.

"John," she whispered. "It was my grandfather's name."

Hank smiled, seeming happy with the choice. Lifting his gaze from their son, he held hers.

"We're parents," he said. "I promise to provide for you and our son."

Betsy nodded. "I know you will," she whispered. "I hope I have the strength to raise him."

Hank put his hand on her cheek. "He'll have an angel for a mother."

May 1937

Hannie was getting married today. The whole family was thrilled, and it felt like the first time her father had truly smiled since their mother's passing. Some said Jesper Baer was proud. He held his head high and didn't often associate with people poorer than he. He had worked all his life to be wealthy, learning to build ships and make a name for himself. Though he'd grown up with little, his family was now among the richest in Zeist.

Sometimes Betsy wondered if he'd forgotten his early years. If people struggled financially, he called them lazy, and he had little faith in those, like her husband, who were trying to make their way as he had.

Jesper had wanted his children to all marry well, but to his dismay the first two had chosen spouses quite below their status. Arend had married a shoemaker's daughter and Betsy had married a preacher's boy.

But finally, Jesper had his heart's desire. His daughter Hannie was engaged to a man of means. A government worker and a lawyer's son, Isaak De Ryke was very well-off.

When the wedding day arrived, the Baer house was astir with preparations. Downstairs the men watched the children and went over last-minute details, and upstairs in Hannie's bedroom the women busily fretted in front of the mirror. Betsy stood braiding and pinning her hair. Their sister-in-law, Angela, slipped into her bridesmaid dress and applied a coat of lipstick. Hannie tried to sit still while Janet unpinned her last few rollers.

"You'll never have a care in the world," Janet said matter-of-factly.

"Except which dress to wear to what party," Angela chimed in.

The girls laughed. Hannie seemed happy, and Betsy was glad. Her sister had dated several men, most of whom her family, not just Father, had disapproved. She certainly had a mind of her own, and Betsy sometimes worried about her.

Hannie had been so young when Mother fell ill that Janet and Betsy had practically raised her. They'd done their best, but she had always pushed against their guidance. Thankfully, from what she knew of him, Isaak was a nice enough young man, and Betsy hoped it would all turn out well.

"Hold still while I do your hair," Janet demanded, running fingers through Hannie's glimmering curls.

"Always the mother hen." Hannie laughed. "In a few hours' time, you'll never be able to boss me around again. And leave some curls down, won't you? I'd hate to look old and prim like you."

"Ha!" Janet scoffed. "Mind your tongue, or I'll get the scissors."

The girls laughed again.

"You'll have to learn to do more for yourself, Hannie," Angela chided. "If Janet can't boss you, I'm sure she won't want to curl your hair."

"I suppose I shall. You'll still help me with my mending. Right, Janet?" Hannie laughed.

Her oldest sister chuckled. "Helping all of you seems to be my fate."

Betsy smiled. Janet *did* do a lot. Recently she'd been watching little John once a week so Betsy could get groceries.

"Is it too much for you, Janet?" Betsy asked.

"It's never too much," Janet retorted. Her sister seemed almost offended at the question. "I'm not a weakling, Betsy."

Betsy bit her lip. She knew her sister meant well, but sometimes her harsh words stung. Janet claimed to be always well, ever strong and completely independent. She helped everyone and yet refused to be coddled herself. Betsy had always envied her sister's strength.

"Are we still going to have our weekly coffee times?" Angela finished buttoning her gown, then slipped on her heels.

"Of course we shall," Hannie piped up. "I may be a successful married woman, but I'll still make time for all of you."

"How thoughtful," Janet quipped. Spraying the ringlets, she turned to Betsy, "I think I hear your baby crying."

Betsy nodded and slipped into the hall. A thousand memories always flooded back as Betsy walked this passage. Pencil marks lined the wall telling of happy children who were now very much grown. Her mother's painting of a windmill hung always a little askew beside their parents' room, and with a lump in her throat Betsy carefully adjusted the frame. She'd always felt safe within these walls. Even when her mother lay dying, Betsy knew she'd always be cared for and belong here. She hoped her own children would feel the same way about their childhood home.

Moving towards her old bedroom, she opened the door and tiptoed inside. Baby John was pushing a year and could now hoist himself to a standing position. He gripped the rails of her old crib and began to smile through his tears. His chubby arms slapped the wooden bars, begging to be picked up.

"Ma… ma…" He grinned, another tooth peeking through his gums. She wrapped her dainty hands around his waist and pulled him close.

"Sweet darling," she whispered.

Within seconds, the boy wriggled to be free. She set him down and he started to crawl towards the open door. Betsy wondered if she'd soon be able to keep up, especially with more than one underfoot. Putting her hand on her abdomen, she smiled faintly. They hadn't anticipated having another so soon, but the Lord had had other plans.

She picked up the child again and carried him downstairs. Perhaps Hank could see to his lunch. She followed voices to the kitchen, where her father and Arend sat drinking coffee at the table. Isaak and the minister were quietly discussing something by the far window, and Arend's children were playing out back.

But her husband was nowhere to be found.

"Where's Hank?" she asked the two at the table.

"I don't keep track of that young man," her father replied coolly, taking a sip of his coffee. "It seems he's always roaming about."

Betsy swallowed hard. She could sometimes brush off his comments, but today it felt more difficult. She'd fallen in love with Hank's adventurous spirit, but even she sometimes longed for a more predictable life. It was a wedding day, after all. Where could he possibly have gone?

Looking for some help, she eyed her brother.

Arend cast a sympathetic look in her direction, then rose from the table to refill his cup. "Hank works hard to provide for Betsy and John. There's no denying the progress he's made at the company. Wouldn't you agree, Father?"

"Taking that job was the smartest thing he's ever done," came her father's cold reply. "I hope he'll stick with it."

Her face flushing, Betsy turned away. She didn't want her father to know how much she agreed with him, how much she worried about the future. Money was tight, and they'd be welcoming their second baby in a few months… another mouth to feed.

She heard her father rise, and he came and stood beside her, speaking softly. "I just want what's best for you."

Putting on a brave face, she turned to him. "Hank *is* what's best for me," she whispered.

She could see her father didn't believe it. He nonetheless nodded, turned, and made his way outside.

Still not knowing where her husband was, she got to feeding her son, spooning as much oatmeal into him as he would allow. When Arend offered to watch him, she let him go free with his cousins and headed back upstairs.

As she opened the bedroom door, she saw Janet buttoning Hannie's gown. How grown up her baby sister looked, and it took her breath away.

"Betsy! We need your opinion!" Angela exclaimed.

Betsy smiled and closed the door behind her.

"I don't think I'll beat Betsy." Hannie giggled. "She's broken the family record, I think."

"What are you talking about?" she asked, sitting down on the bed, trying to forget her worries.

"How long, Betsy?" Angela asked. "How long till Isaak and Hannie are expecting? I say a month. Janet says at least three."

Betsy laughed. "I couldn't begin to guess."

"I hope having a baby doesn't make me fat." Hannie frowned. "I do so care about my figure." With a glimmer of pride, Hannie ran her palms down her bodice.

Betsy couldn't ignore her sister's trim waist, and she instinctively put a hand on her own belly. Having babies took its toll on a woman's body and she had tried her best to accept that fact.

There was a knock at the door and Jesper's voice called to them, "The car is leaving in ten minutes! You girls ready?"

Hannie looked frantic. "We still have to put on my veil and brooch and... Isaak certainly mustn't see me!"

"Stop fussing," Janet scolded unsympathetically. "I heard Isaak and the minister head out a few minutes ago, and we have plenty of time for your accessories." She turned to Betsy. "Tell Father we'll be along shortly."

Betsy did as she was told. Opening the door, she delivered the message to her father. "Is Hank downstairs?" she then asked.

Though seemingly frustrated by the question, her father withheld any harsh words. "He came in just before I came up. Said he was at his shop."

Biting her lip, she nodded and looked into her father's keen eyes, searching for some measure of understanding. "I hope you'll grow to love Hank... and see what a good man he is."

Her father shrugged. "I'm glad you're happy."

Not one to show affection, Jespar surprised her by touching her arm. It was the smallest gesture, but Betsy felt the weight of it. Then, just as quickly, he turned and made his way to the stairs, calling behind him.

"And you've got a fine little boy down there. I think he looks like me."

Taking a deep breath, Betsy smiled.

Her father headed back downstairs and she returned to her sisters. They had picked up their previous conversation while Janet pinned the veil in place.

"If you do find out you're expecting, Hannie," Janet declared, "you better tell us immediately. Don't make us guess like Betsy did."

Hannie laughed. "You know I will. We Baer girls don't keep secrets."

Chapter Eight

July 1937

"I won't be able to do this come August," Betsy whispered to herself, quietly shutting John's nursery door.

Thankfully her little son still napped, which gave her ample time for a music lesson. It had been over a year since Diederik had offered to teach her piano, and she had finally worked up the courage to learn. She had always wanted to play an instrument but never thought herself able. Hannie was the musical one of the family. From a young age, her sister had played piano and violin, and she sang like a bird. Betsy had always felt outshone by her and, if she were honest, intimidated by her talent.

So she'd settled for taking care of the little ones and baking her favourite sweets. People raved about her spritskoeken, until her mother had warned her against eating too many sweets.

"They'll make you sick, my dear. I've lived with this nasty disease for a long time, and my doctor says sugar is nothing but gas on the fire."

Betsy had obeyed, like she always did, but deep down inside she longed to try her hand at something, something all her own, something at which people would marvel. She wanted to be more than sweet Betsy. Perhaps she could be a concert pianist.

"Listen to yourself," she murmured with a laugh. "You have all of four weeks before this baby is born. How much can you learn in a month?"

There was a knock at the door and Betsy opened it. The little neighbour girl, Carolein, met her on the porch before stepping inside.

The girl grinned shyly.

"John just went down for his nap, so he should be asleep until I return," Betsy said. "If he wakes, I've left a bottle in the refrigerator. You remember how I showed you to warm it?"

Carolein nodded. "Yes."

"Thanks again." Betsy waved before heading out.

The day was hot, so she was thankful for the short walk next door. Diederik opened the door, as if he'd been watching for her.

"Come, come."

He didn't bother with pleasantries. Whether it was his lack of hearing or matter-of-fact nature, Diederik was always straight to the point.

She followed him inside and slipped off her coat. Hanging it on the peg as she was accustomed to doing, the two made their way to the instrument. He'd placed a few books on top and he motioned for her to sit.

"I thought we'd start with note names." He held up a large music book. The cover was yellowed and stained, the spine worn and the pages folded here and there. "It's been so long since I looked at these books. I forgot I had them."

Betsy watched the elderly man lovingly thumb through the pages.

"Let me sit and show you," he commanded.

She slid across the bench, absent-mindedly holding her belly. She was bigger this time than last and nervous because of it. John's birth had been hard, and the midwife had confirmed this baby was probably even bigger.

Diederik played a few notes and called out each by name. Betsy watched and listened closely, committing them to memory.

"Play with feeling," he told her. "You should hear each distinct note."

She followed his lead.

"Play with confidence… that's it…"

When the lesson was over, Betsy glanced at the worn hymnal left untouched on a nearby shelf. "I wish I could play those songs. They mean so very much to me."

Even as she spoke, the familiar words repeated themselves in her heart: *"Fear not, I am with thee, oh, be not dismayed"*

"Ah. You will learn them soon enough." The old gentleman patted her arm. "It just takes practice."

"I'm afraid I haven't long for that." Betsy dropped her head. "When this baby comes, I'll have no time for lessons."

Diederik cupped his hand to his ear. "You've got to speak up, young lady."

"I won't have time once the baby comes," Betsy spoke louder. "I only have four weeks to learn."

"Nonsense." Diederik waved his hand as if swatting a fly. "That's not enough time at all! Just bring the baby with you. I don't mind a little one. It'll bring life to the place."

Betsy smiled. She could try, but every thought of having two little ones made her weary and her chest hurt.

"I don't think I have what it takes to raise two," she confided.

Though Diederik struggled to hear and wasn't always very observant, he saw the apprehension in her eyes. Betsy knew he did.

"Then you'll have to get a nanny, someone to help you."

Betsy hadn't even thought of that, but she shook her head. "We couldn't afford it," she mumbled.

Diederik thought for a moment. "Don't worry about costs. I'll ask Eliana to come over and help you. Agreed?"

The man's forwardness and generosity amazed her. She hardly knew what to say, and she wondered how Hank would respond. He was a good man but proud.

"I don't know…" Betsy stammered. "That's far too generous."

"Ah!" Diederik exclaimed. "Doesn't the Lord promise to help us in trouble? Take it as a gift from him."

Betsy tried to form a reply, but she was at a loss. Perhaps the Lord was keeping his promise.

"For I am thy God, and will still give thee aid."

August 1937

Baby Henry arrived. He was big, beautiful, and sweet, but Betsy and her husband had their work cut out for them. The long nights up with the baby proved to be extra exhausting the second time around. While John usually slept through the night, he was awake most of the day. Between her two sons' schedules, Betsy had hardly any time to rest.

But today was the day. Diederik was sending Eliana over to meet the boys. Betsy had been grateful for the man's help but hadn't been sure how Hank would respond. Diederik was offering to pay the nanny's wage, somewhat like charity. Hank *had* refused at first, but when Diederik had pressed the matter, explaining that Eliana came from a poor family and needed more work than he could supply, Hank acquiesced.

"I'm sure I'll make more money soon," Hank promised. "Then we can pay her ourselves."

The young lady would only come twice a week for a few hours at a time, long enough for Betsy to either go to her piano lesson, have a rest, or do the shopping.

"Thank you, Lord," she whispered, finishing up the breakfast dishes.

The baby was down for his nap while little John played at her feet, trying to stack a block with all the precision and determination a one-year-old could muster. Sticking out his tongue was how he focused, and his little pudgy fingers did their best to be careful.

Hanging up her tea towel, she smiled. "Stack the tower, John. That's it."

He laid the second block and to her amazement a third, and then, with just as much resolve as he'd had in building it, used his forearm to knock it to the ground. Not yet content with the mess, he kicked the blocks further across the room, smiling and squealing in delight.

"Shh…" Betsy smiled and bent down to his level, hoping Henry would sleep through the chaos. She was still learning to care for boys, for it didn't come naturally. Being so soft-spoken herself and having only one brother so close in age, Betsy hadn't had much experience rearing little boys. Even the children she'd cared for as a nanny were all little girls. "Give me patience," she often prayed.

"Come now, John," she coaxed. "Let's pick up your blocks."

"No!"

There was a knock at the door and John scrambled to his feet. Though he'd been walking for a while, he had found a new fascination for outrunning his mother. He beat her to the door and tried to reach the handle. He was a tall toddler, but not yet tall enough to reach the latch.

Betsy opened the door and the young woman met her. She had a serious expression, though her eyes betrayed kindness.

"Hello," Betsy greeted, ushering her inside.

While he'd been confident a moment ago, John now hid behind her leg and begged to be held. Gathering him into her arms, she invited the girl to sit.

"I'm eager to start working for you," Eliana said. "I worked as a nanny for a few years before Mr. Vanderhoof took me on. I can give you a list of references."

Betsy herself was not always outgoing with strangers. Like her son, she sometimes grew shy in their presence. "Diederik speaks very highly of you."

Eliana smiled. "This is your eldest, I presume?"

"Yes." She smiled at her chubby son who'd nestled his face in her neck.

Knowing he was being spoken about, he poked his head out and tried to hide a smile creeping to his lips.

Eliana eyed the toys behind them and pointed. "Do show me your blocks," she invited him, and that was all the boy needed. He wriggled down from Betsy's arms, but rather than run away he clasped Betsy's hand and pulled her towards them.

Just then, Betsy heard baby Henry. He'd hardly slept twenty minutes, and her heart sank, exhausted.

Her weariness must've shown, for Eliana quickly offered, "Allow me."

Betsy pointed towards the baby room and Eliana made quick work. She opened the door and tiptoed inside. Gathering the bundle, she rocked him back and forth before bringing him to the kitchen.

"What a sweet soul," she mused, looking up at Betsy. "But a tired one."

Betsy wondered if she was talking about the baby or the mother.

"Do *you* have children?" Betsy wanted to know.

"No, but I've got many young siblings. And though I never had children of my own, I've learned a lot caring for them…" Eliana shifted the baby to her shoulder and rubbed his bottom. "…like how this baby needs a change right away."

Betsy took the child while Eliana offered to help John with his tower.

After changing the baby, she offered the girl some coffee. "Diederik says you attend church together."

Eliana nodded. "The little white chapel on Fortieth."

"You don't go to synagogue?" Betsy queried. Diederik had confirmed Betsy's assumption that the girl was Jewish.

Eliana shook her head. "My parents are believers. We honour our Jewish heritage, but we know the true Messiah."

Betsy marvelled.

"They're wonderful people… at the chapel," Eliana went on. "I've grown a lot thanks to Reverend Laanstra's preaching. When I'm sitting in church, I feel how much God loves me."

Betsy wondered whether *she* had grown while going to church. She knew God, and she loved him, but she wondered if there was more to discover. He'd certainly gotten her through hardships and shown himself to be good, but perhaps he was even better than she thought. She knew he was strong, but could he help her withstand even greater storms? As for church, she felt closer to God in her garden or listening to Diederik's piano playing than sitting in a pew.

"Does John like books?" Eliana wondered.

Betsy could hardly respond before John had up and toddled to his stack. The girl began to read and John laughed with glee. Eliana was so good with him that Betsy started to feel intimidated. *She* was the mother, and yet this woman seemed so confident, so good at everything.

Eliana must've read her expression, so before she left she put a hand on Betsy's arm and offered a smile. "You're a good mother," she whispered, and with that she was gone.

Chapter Nine

April 1938

While Hank didn't attend church most Sundays, today was Easter, and he'd promised he would. On Saturday night, Betsy had bathed the boys and ensured they had enough bread and milk in the fridge, so all they had to do the next morning was dress, eat and walk to church.

Reverend Vischer, Hank's father, would be preaching as usual today, and then they were to have dinner with his parents and brother. Hank would have refused the invitation had not Betsy stepped in.

"It's Easter, my love," she said. "And they've barely seen baby Henry since he was born."

Hank had finally consented.

Betsy hoped their visit would go well. Except when at church, Betsy had hardly seen the Vischers since they were married. Hank had never had a good relationship with his father, and his mother and brother did everything his father wished. Betsy had heard through the grapevine that Bram still didn't have enough money to attend seminary; no matter how much he wanted to please his father, he struggled to hold a steady job. It seemed Bram had a few too many "bad days" for any employer to overlook.

Reverend Vischer often tried to smooth things over, but Betsy wondered if he only made things worse. It seemed his expectations had, though in different ways, only served to hurt his children. Hank's carefree and adventurous ways had clashed with his father's proper ones, and he'd spent his whole life resenting him for it. On the other hand, Bram's compliance and people-pleasing had made him indecisive and overly dependent on others.

Once dressed and fed, Hank, Betsy, and the boys headed out into the April morning. The sun was warm and the trees were beginning to bud. The smell of hyacinths perfumed the air and Betsy hoped the lovely day would calm her anxious heart.

Hank held little John as they meandered down the sidewalk, sometimes letting him down to run ahead while Betsy pushed the baby in the carriage. The infant was sleeping soundly, usually a good thing, but Betsy feared it meant he'd be awake and fussy during the service.

As they walked, John chatted and explored the world around him, and her husband engaged him cheerfully. Betsy missed the days when she and Hank would talk more, but things were now starting to feel distant between them.

Hank had been so busy at the company, and Betsy had thought *that* the reason for the disconnect. She'd begged him to take a few days off, and he'd complied.

However, things hadn't gotten better. At times, Hank felt a hundred miles away.

Was it worry that distracted her husband? They still struggled to make ends meet. Though her father had generously offered more work on the weekends, Hank preferred to use that time to tinker. Betsy hadn't minded his decision, but as prices rose she felt a growing resentment. Hank told her everything would be fine, but Betsy saw the worry written all over, the tension between doing what he loved and doing his duty.

To add to their anxieties, Germany was on the move. She'd heard Hank talking to Arend and Isaak about their recent annexation of Austria. What would they do next? Hopefully nothing more.

They came in view of the church and Betsy tried to push away her worries and think about something else. Today they would partake in communion. Though it'd never meant much to her before, she secretly hoped today would be different.

Eliana's words echoed in her heart: *When I'm sitting in church, I feel how much God loves me.*

Had she ever felt that? She knew it wasn't all about feelings. Hadn't Reverend Vischer often quoted "The heart is deceitful above all things" more times than she could count? She knew her feelings often let her down, taking her to places that were unhealthy and unhelpful. But it'd been so long since she'd felt wonderful. Though her babies were dear, she felt that tiredness and frustration often inhibited her from enjoying them as much as she could.

"Lord, I want to feel you," she whispered. Was it too much to ask?

Reaching the church steps, she lifted her sleeping baby from the carriage, hoping he wouldn't wake. He did.

Her husband ushered her in and then took John to the men's side. Betsy caught sight of her sisters and joined them in their pew.

Reverend Vischer began the service, but Betsy was too tired to focus. While baby Henry seemed content for now, she could see that John was busy. First he climbed over Hank. Then he wanted to run down the aisle.

After what seemed like only a few minutes, Hank took John by the hand and quickly walked him out, his frustration palpable.

Reverend Vischer eyed her more than once. His gaze was not condemning, but neither was it kind. Betsy felt horrible.

So much for wanting to feel God. She just wanted to go home.

The service pressed on, but a moment later Henry began to cry again—hungry. Janet turned and gave her a sympathetic look, but she was also quick to motion her away. This was not acceptable church behaviour.

As quietly as she could, Betsy slipped out of the service.

What an embarrassment. Did other women struggle like she did? Many mothers brought their children to church, and Betsy thought she'd never seen such a disturbance like what her own boys had caused that morning. She held the baby close to her bosom and scanned the churchyard for her husband. Where could he have gone?

Frustration welled up uninvited. Her cheeks burned, even as the baby's cry escalated. She had to get home, but where was Hank? Had he gone home without her?

She was exhausted, utterly worn out. Her head ached and she had to get this baby fed.

Hands fumbling, she lay the screaming child in his carriage. She had better just go.

"Hush, dear," she tried to whisper, but her words felt forced and anything but soothing.

They started down the sidewalk, the sun warming her back and making her perspire. It was almost noon and she felt hungry. Clenching her jaw, she tried to contain some of her anger.

When they arrived home, Hank was nowhere to be found. She took the crying baby and tried to nurse, but he was so worked up that he didn't latch.

"Come on, my son," she pleaded.

Tears blurred her vision and she couldn't easily make out his fair features that were so like his father's. His blond hair was already thick with a few curls. His light skin had a rosy glow, and his eyes were big... just like Hank's.

But where *was* her husband? Betsy didn't know whether to yell or cry. The baby's resistance was making her panic, and her body began to tremble. She was famished, thirsty, and tired.

Suddenly the door opened, and there was her husband and toddler son. Hank banged the door shut.

"Why didn't you tell me you were going home?" Hank asked. "I waited outside for an hour."

Betsy realized he must have gone around back and she had just missed him. There was no stopping the sobs now, and Betsy dropped her head, feeling the weight of everything crush her. She was too tired to be indignant, to make any smart comment about how she'd looked for him as well. She was exhausted and her body was succumbing to its weariness.

In a moment, Betsy felt baby Henry being lifted from her arms. He was still crying, still too hungry to eat and too sleepy to sleep. How she could relate.

She felt her husband's strong arms encircle her, his warm scent a familiar comfort.

"Mama crying…" John whimpered, wriggling between his parents' embrace.

Betsy lifted her head to look at the child. She planted a soft kiss on his forehead. "Mama's fine," she said. "Just tired."

"Why?" John wanted to know. It was his favourite question of late.

"Your Mama works hard," Hank replied, his voice deep and full of feeling.

Content with his answer, John managed his escape and ran to play with his toys. Her husband had miraculously managed to soothe the baby's cries ever so slightly, and it proved enough to get him to latch. He began to eat while Betsy tried to keep her eyes open.

When the child was finished and asleep, she carried him to his crib. Setting him down, she at once felt her husband beside her again. This time, his arms encircled her waist and turned her towards himself. Hand under her chin, he met her weary gaze with his own.

"I'm sorry for my harsh words, Betsy, and for not being there when you needed me. It's just that I've had a lot on my mind… the world… the future… our family… I'm sorry."

It seemed all her tears had been spent. Betsy leaned her forehead against her husband's shoulder and exhaled.

"I am too," she whispered.

"Why should you be sorry? You're an angel, Betsy. A perfect angel."

Betsy shook her head. She knew she was not. She knew the resentment and self-pity that so often rose to the surface. She knew the assumptions and disrespect she had undeservedly awarded her husband. And yet he was so kind.

She wrapped her arms around his neck and quickly felt sleep overtake her. Her husband must've noticed. Pulling her into his arms, he carried her to their bed and laid her down.

"Your parents… dinner…" Betsy could barely make out the words.

"Not to worry," he whispered, kissing her brow. "We aren't expected for another few hours." Tucking a whisp of hair behind her ear, he added spitefully, "My father's sermon will be long today."

As she was drifting off, she heard his final words.

"Rest, dear wife. It seems even angels need their sleep."

♪♫♪

Betsy awoke and slipped from the covers, thankful for a couple hours of sleep. Glancing in the mirror, she sighed at the wrinkly dress she'd planned to wear to lunch. The pale pink smock was her best gown reserved for Sundays, but now it was far from appropriate. Something else would have to do.

Changing into a clean dress, she splashed some cool water on her face and pinned a few stray hairs.

Her husband met her in the kitchen. "You ready?"

Nodding, she placed Henry in the baby carriage and the four headed out.

It was a short walk to the Vischers' family home, and when they arrived Mrs. Vischer greeted them at the door. Taking their coats, she quietly led them into the dining room. Dessert and coffee were first on the menu; everything was already prepared. They made their way to the table where Reverend Vischer and Bram sat waiting. It seemed they were late after all.

Hank and Betsy sat down, John on his father's knee and baby Henry asleep in his carrying basket.

Mrs. Vischer poured the coffee, and they began to eat.

"How's work going?" Hank asked his brother.

"I gave my resignation yesterday."

"Oh?"

"Going to seminary this fall."

"You finally can do it?"

Reverend Vischer bristled, spearing a piece of cake and bringing it to his mouth. "Bram has been wanting to attend seminary for years. We… that is, he… just had to save enough money."

Now it was Hank's turn to bristle. "You're putting him through?"

Reverend Vischer cleaned his plate and looked his oldest son straight in the eye. "That is none of your concern, Henry. What we do with our money is none of your concern."

"This is very good cake," Betsy blurted out.

Her mother-in-law nodded a thank-you.

"What will you be doing over the summer?" Hank asked his brother.

"I'll be sticking around here." Bram tried to look confident. "Father has some odd jobs he needs help with. And I'll be picking up more work at the ice cream parlour."

"What kind of odd jobs?" Hank pushed back from the table. "I didn't hear about this."

"That is also none of your concern." Reverend Vischer looked like he might pounce. "Bram will be helping me repair a few things... that's all."

At this, John wriggled from his father's arms, wanting to play. Mrs. Vischer retrieved a few toys for him. Thankful for the diversion, Betsy excused herself to watch him. There were too many breakable things to let him go unattended.

"Bram isn't a repairman," she heard her husband mutter, taking a sip of his coffee. Why couldn't he just let it go?

"I'm sure you think you could do better." The reverend glared at his eldest son. "I'm sure you *could* do better if you tried."

Mrs. Vischer cleared the plates, seeming anxious to move things along.

Baby Henry awoke and Betsy went to him, leaving John in his father's care. A horrible smell wafted from his diaper and she pulled a clean one from her bag, listening as she worked.

"I saw you leave services early." Reverend Vischer's voice was low.

Her husband sighed. "You forget how hard it is with young children."

"I remember. I see your wife managing them alone every Sunday..."

Their words trailed off as Betsy's anxiety rose.

She set a blanket down on the ground and laid her son on top. His chubby hands clapped happily and he tried to wriggle away. At eight months old, he was rolling and chattering all the time.

When she returned to the table, Mrs. Vischer had set out the roast and Bram had helped her with the vegetables.

Reverend Vischer was still speaking. "The Bible warns…" he cleared his throat. "…against forsaking the assembling of ourselves together, as the manner of *some* is."[2]

"Haven't you preached enough today?" Hank retorted, his fist clenched in his lap.

Betsy sat down and tried to take his hand.

"But you are dull of hearing," his father prodded.

Betsy couldn't take any more. She turned to her mother-in-law. "Perhaps we should eat," she whispered. "The roast smells delicious."

The woman nodded and brought over a steaming pot of potatoes.

"We shall partake." Reverend Vischer nodded, then turned to Hank with a smirk. "Will you pray for us?"

This was the last straw. Her husband stood and turned to Betsy. "We best be going."

---

[2] See Hebrews 10:24.

Chapter Ten

December 1938

It was St. Nicholas Day, Betsy's favourite time of year. The holidays were especially fun with two little boys. Their wonder and anticipation made her feel like a child herself. John was two and a half and Henry about a year younger. Though they were no help at this age, Betsy had shown them how to make *speculaas*. She'd also cut out paper snowflakes and let them colour them, after which they tied them with thread and hung them on the tree.

She and Hank didn't have money for presents this year, and Betsy had tried to put on a brave face about it.

"The boys are too young to know any difference," she'd told her husband with a smile.

But while that may be true, Betsy knew Hank was embarrassed because of it. Her family would spoil them with toys of all kinds; she and Hank would have nothing elaborate to give. The boys would be elated with everything, but the parents would feel terrible.

Celebrations would begin in just a few hours. Betsy had two pies in the oven and Henry would be getting up from his nap shortly. Hank was finishing up a project in the shop.

John played happily with his tin soldiers by the sofa. Ever since Uncle Arend had gotten him the toys for his birthday, John had been obsessed with playing army. Though she hadn't said anything, Betsy didn't appreciate the gift. She'd grown up hearing stories about the Great War. Her teachers had planned lessons around the different battles, and her parents had openly thanked God that the Netherlands had remained neutral. Some children found the stories thrilling, but Betsy never liked them. They always made her uneasy.

Smells of cinnamon and nutmeg brought her back to the present and made her mouth water. Retrieving a clean bottle from the cupboard, she filled it with milk, then pulled the pies from the oven.

"Mum!" John had toddled to her side. "I want a cookie!"

"You'll have plenty of sweets at Opa's, my boy. I'll get you some fruit!"

The boy crossed his arms, pouting. "No!"

Rubbing her temples, Betsy felt a headache coming on. She'd had several migraines recently, and that was unusual. While she tried not to let it bother her, it did. It felt impossible not to worry or jump to conclusions.

Crouching down to his level, Betsy took the boy's hand. "Would you like applesauce?"

A smile crept onto his lips and she filled him a bowl.

When Baby Henry woke a few minutes later, Hank appeared from the work shed. They all headed out to the vehicle as a few snowflakes began to fall. It was a short but lovely ride to the Baer home.

Delicious smells greeted them as they ascended the front steps and let themselves in. A dozen stockings hung over the fire and a bowl of red and white candy canes sat proudly on the coffee table. Already the house was bustling. Arend, Isaak, and her father sat in the living room, deep in conversation.

Hank delivered the pies to the kitchen and then sat down with the men in the living room. Betsy worked at getting the boys out of their coats. She didn't usually like the men's conversations, but today she couldn't help overhearing them.

"I hear Levy will have to sell his business over in Berlin," Arend declared.

Her father shook his head. "Forced to, more like it. He's one of my oldest suppliers."

"Thirty years." Arend nodded knowingly.

"Will you be able to keep working with them?" Isaak queried. "Whoever takes it over?"

Jespar Baer laughed. "Not if they're some German corporation. Levy built that company from the ground up just to have it all taken away by some Nazi thieves."

"We might have to work with them," Arend said, trying to be reasonable. "They're one of our biggest partners."

"I'm not teaming up with those scoundrels." Her father slammed his fist down on the coffee table, rattling his cup and saucer. "Levy is more than a partner. He is my friend."

"He's a Jew," Isaak muttered under his breath.

Her father's eyes flashed. "One of the best of them."

"We might still be able to work with these people," Arend suggested.

"Over my dead body." And with that, her father ended the conversation.

Having gotten the boys out of their jackets and hats, Betsy ushered them towards the kitchen, finding John a playmate on the way. As she entered with Henry, she saw Janet stirring something at the stove.

"Your pies look good." Her sister didn't look up.

Betsy smiled, feeling an ounce of pride. Mouth watering, she eyed the table full of food. An impressive assortment of meats, vegetables, and sauces sat there, just ready to be consumed. Janet always outdid herself during the holidays. The dinner was meant to be a team effort—Betsy baking pies, Angela bringing *oliebollen*, and Hannie cooking some sort of vegetable. But Janet not only cooked the roast but made a scrumptious *stamppot*, mashing vegetables and seasoning the meat to perfection. Her gravy and other sauces were thick and flavourful, and she always made sure to bake lots of *pepernoten* cookies for the children, of which there were many. It seemed every year more babies were added to the Baer clan. Arend and Angela had welcomed a third in September. She and Hank had their two, and Isaak and Hannie just had their first last month... six in all, and Betsy was sure there were more to come.

"It smells divine." She came to stand by her sister, bouncing babbling Henry on her hip.

"It'd better. I've been slaving away since yesterday morning." Setting down her spoon and turning off the stove, Janet turned and faced her. "You don't look well."

Even in the middle of sheer chaos, she couldn't keep a secret from her sister.

"I'm fine," she fibbed.

"Don't you dare lie to me," Janet warned, hands on her hips, love in her eyes.

"My head just hurts. That's all."

"It *is* loud in here." Hannie sighed, entering the kitchen and joining the conversation uninvited. Cradling her baby in her arms, she pushed back a stray hair. With trim waist, blond curls, and creamy smooth skin, Hannie was still the picture of youth. She turned to her eldest sister. "Would you mind watching Ferdi? I really must do something with this hair."

Not waiting for a response, she dropped the baby in Janet's arms and left the room as quickly as she'd entered.

Janet rolled her eyes. Hannie was always leaning on her for help. In truth, they all did. Janet played the role of mother well. And even though she had her father's personality, Betsy had never realized how closely Janet resembled their mother.

"I miss Mother," she whispered, just loud enough for her sister to hear.

Understanding, Janet nodded. "The holidays will do that."

"I often think back to the last time I spoke with her. I told her how alone I felt. I didn't feel God with me. I didn't feel any peace. Did I ever tell you what she said?"

"No," Janet replied, tapping her spoon clean and moving the last pot to the table. Though she feigned disinterest, Betsy knew she was listening.

"She said, 'You're never alone.'"

Janet turned to look at her, rocking Ferdi as he began to whimper. "'Never will I leave you. Never will I forsake you,'"[3] she quoted.

"Sometimes I don't feel that's true," Betsy whispered. "I don't feel God close to me."

"It doesn't matter what you feel, Betsy."

Betsy dropped her gaze.

---

[3] See Hebrews 13:5.

"I'm sorry," Janet was quick to say. "I suppose feelings have their place. I wish I had half the sensitivity you do."

"Maybe then we'd balance each other out," Betsy said, chuckling.

Janet laughed too, then poured a cup of coffee. "Drink some of this, Betsy. It'll help your head."

Betsy took the warm cup gratefully.

The Baer family celebration had come and gone. Hank, Betsy, and their two tired but happy sons returned home. With the boys in bed and a small fire in the hearth, Hank took her in his arms.

"How are you, my angel?" He pulled her close.

"Tired," she whispered.

Though she loved her family dearly, she'd felt the tension among them. Hank was growing restless at the company. He'd mentioned quitting more than once and Jespar had gotten wind of it. She'd seen her father's disapproval of him many times that day. He'd watched silently as the children opened gifts. While Arend's children got store-bought dolls and trains, and even Hannie's baby got brand-new blankets and rattles, John and Henry opened handmade trinkets. Betsy had sewn them tiny animals and stuffed them with old rags. She'd filled their little stockings with bags of dried fruit and nuts. But it all paled in comparison to the gifts the other children got.

Betsy was thankful the boys were too young to notice, but she knew her father did.

Jespar pulled Betsy aside after the gifts had been opened and whispered, "I'm sorry for your plight, Betsy, and I'm concerned that Hank won't make enough to provide for you. Perhaps you can talk Hank out of leaving the company. I'm willing to give him a raise if he'll stay on."

Betsy had felt torn. Her father was being generous and kind, but she knew her husband was discontent. "Hank loves working on radios, father," she had replied. "You know he's not a shipbuilder."

"But he could work on parts. He's knowledgeable. I'll give him that."

It was the kindest word he had ever said about her husband.

"What was your father talking to you about earlier?" Hank now asked, ushering her back to the present.

"He said…" Should she tell him? She knew Hank would stay on if she ever asked him to. "He said… he'd give you a raise if you stayed on."

Pulling away, Hank grew quiet.

The fire crackled as another log burst into flames. Betsy watched the amber glow, wondering whether Hank would even consider the offer.

"Is that what you want me to do?" he asked seriously.

"You should do… what you want to do."

In truth, she'd love to have more money, enough to buy nice Christmas gifts for the children, enough for a few extra groceries and a few more clothes.

Unfortunately, her husband was good at reading between the lines. "But you want me to work with your father."

There was a sharpness in his voice, and she knew she'd struck a nerve.

She dropped her gaze. "I shouldn't have brought it up."

"Your father brought it up," her husband replied coolly. "He wishes I was like your brother Arend or Hannie's new husband. He wishes I were wealthy, or at least trying to be." Anger rose with every word. "It seems money is all that man thinks about."

Betsy hated seeing him angry, but now she was too. Surely Hank was being unfair. Her father was a good man. But the two of them were so very different. Would it really be so bad to have more money? To have a new dress or two? To have store-bought Christmas gifts?

"We'll be fine, Hank," she whispered. "I shouldn't be so selfish."

"No. You could never be selfish."

Hank never seemed to see her flaws, but Betsy knew better. She'd eyed Hannie's fine dress today and Angela's earrings. Even Janet, who was too sensible for high fashion, had donned a new silk shirt and cuffs. Betsy wished she hadn't noticed, but she had. She wished she didn't care about such things.

Her husband took her hand. "I wish I could just stay on, Betsy. I wish I could be satisfied with that. But the world is changing… and people need to stay informed. Radio… it's my passion."

Betsy put her arms around his neck and drew a deep breath. "I'm sorry," she whispered into his shirt. Wasn't this why she loved him? His passion? His courage? "I support you in whatever you choose. You're a good husband and a good father."

Hank shook his head. "You don't know what it means to hear you say so."

Kissing her, he rose and moved towards the tree, where he produced a small box. She hadn't noticed it nestled behind the branches.

"What's that?" she asked, thankful for a diversion.

"It's your gift."

Betsy didn't feel like getting a gift, not when she'd been so shallow a moment ago. "Where did you get the money?"

"What money?" He grinned. "Open it."

Taking the box, she loosened the bow and pulled off the lid. She gasped. It was her beloved radio that Hank had given her years ago, beautifully polished and looking like new.

"Turn it on," Hank encouraged.

"But the boys…"

Hank adjusted the knob. "It'll be quiet."

Turning it on, she found it was tuned to the local station. A soft melody caught her ear and she smiled.

O Holy Night
The stars are brightly shining.
It is the night of our dear Savior's birth.

"Care to dance, my angel?" Her husband offered his hand.

Nodding, Betsy stood, enveloped in his arms.

Long lay the world in sin and e'er pining
'Til He appeared and the soul felt its worth.

And the final bit.

A thrill of hope the weary world rejoices
For yonder breaks a new and glorious morn.[4]

How weary she did feel, dancing in the firelight. She didn't feel God, and she didn't feel good. But because of Jesus, she was learning that she had something greater than happy feelings.

Hope.

---

[4] Placide Cappeau, "O Holy Night," 1843.

Chapter Eleven

September 1939

The Germans invaded Poland. What had just been gossip and speculation was now a reality.

Hank sat motionless by his radio, listening. Though he had recently quit the company and had a long list of appliances to fix, he didn't move an inch towards the workshop today. The boys, contentedly unaware, were playing at the big oak table, drawing pictures of trees and plants and new species of animals. Betsy sat with them, trying to encourage them not to draw on the table itself, though her efforts proved fruitless.

She wished she didn't have to, but she heard every word the news reporter spoke.

"Is this war? I suppose time will tell," came the voice.

War. Even the thought of it made her stomach hurt. Her husband had felt worried these last months. Germany had been on the move, but this caught everyone off-guard. What would it all mean?

The report ended. Hank switched off the radio and Betsy moved to the living room. Her husband sat, looking at his hands, lost in thought.

Sitting down beside him, she touched his arm.

"You heard all that?" he asked.

She nodded. "What does it all mean? Is it war like he said?"

Hank shook his head. "No, at least nothing that concerns us right now."

Though her husband spoke confidently, his voice betrayed him. He was worried, as was she.

Though it was a warm September day, Betsy shivered. "I'm afraid," she whispered, not wanting the boys to hear.

Hank took her in his arms. "Don't be. We managed to stay out of one war, and we will again."

Betsy nodded. Her father had always said the Dutch had avoided much heartache and financial loss because of their neutrality in the Great War.

"What about other countries?" she asked.

Hank grew quiet. She knew the matter weighed on him, much heavier than he let on. He chewed over the question for quite some time before turning to face her.

"It's none of our concern right now." He smiled, but it didn't reach his eyes.

He wanted to shield her, to protect her from reality. It seemed Hank wanted everyone else to know the brutal truth except her.

"Mama..."

Their two-year-old son Henry appeared. Holding out his picture, he looked for approval.

Trying to pull herself from her worries, Betsy smiled at the dozen lines and circles etched across the page. "It's beautiful. What is it?"

"A *hoarse*." He beamed with pride.

She smiled. "A fine horse."

Satisfied with her commendation, the little boy ran back to join his brother. Betsy turned and looked back at her husband, but he was again lost in thought, lost in the what-ifs, calculating possibilities she couldn't begin to imagine.

Betsy felt uneasy. But as she was learning to find her strength in God, she prayed.

♪♫♪

"Germany is out of control," Jespar barked, slamming the door behind him. Betsy had stopped by to deliver fresh bread to Janet, but her father had met her on the steps. "They're taking what doesn't belong to them, with no respect for the innocent."

Betsy handed the loaf to her sister. She had never seen her father so angry.

"Why don't you sit down, Father?" Janet coaxed. "I can cut you a slice of Betsy's bread. It still feels warm."

Jespar didn't seem to hear her. Pacing back and forth, he muttered to himself. "They're bombing hospitals… hospitals! Targeting the defenceless. I'm glad Britain and France are taking action."

Thankful her boys were with Eliana and didn't have to hear this, Betsy approached her father. "Do you think… Germany will attack the Netherlands?" She could barely say the words.

"Over my dead body," Jespar huffed, plunking down at the table, looking defeated.

He then turned to his daughters, his gaze looking miles away.

"I could never live in such circumstances," he whispered. "Everyone deserves freedom. I've worked hard for what I have, and no one… I mean, no one will take that from me."

Betsy nodded. It was true: her father had worked his way up from the bottom. He'd built a business and a life and a family from almost nothing. She prayed it would never be stolen away.

January 1, 1940

Elizabeth. It was her mother's name, her name, and now it would be her daughter's too.

Betsy had always found it special to have her mother's name. It was a legacy she'd treasured all her life. While many regarded God as harsh and mean, her mother had spoken something different over her daughter. Some people lived in constant fear, legalistic and duty-obsessed, but her mother hadn't. Even in her sickness, Mrs. Baer had exuded a lightness that attracted her daughter. Betsy hadn't always known what it was, but in recent years she'd come to understand. It was her mother's view of God. To her, he wasn't stiff, mean, and unkind. He had more than enough to give, more than enough love to bestow, more than enough power to keep the world in his hands—no matter how dark things got.

Betsy had always wanted to be like her mother, and she treasured sharing her name. It felt like a little part of her that was all her own.

And now it would belong to her daughter too.

Unlike her brothers, baby Elizabeth was a petite little girl with the loveliest golden hair Betsy had ever seen. The pregnancy too had been different. Betsy had been sicker and more bedridden during her confinement than she had in the previous two.

After the delivery, her midwife Mina had pulled her aside. "I don't think your body can handle another, Betsy. I know you've spoken of having four, but I think it'd be too much."

Betsy knew she was right. Though she had always wanted four, she was content. Her children were truly a blessing from God and she would steward them faithfully. She would raise them in the faith and pray for their souls. She would protect them too as long as she could. She would try to make their home a sanctuary of peace, but she feared the world would come knocking.

She felt it already had. After the invasion of Poland, both France and Britain had declared war on Germany. Not much had affected them yet, but Hank was uneasy. Would the Netherlands get involved? Some people said so. But was it just hearsay? Betsy wanted to believe it was. The idea of war scared her more than anything. Hadn't her family had enough tragedy?

May 1940

"Betsy!"

She'd never heard Janet so distraught. Betsy pushed the receiver closer to her ear. "What is it? What's wrong?"

"It's Father..." Her sister's words trailed off. Betsy heard static, and then she spoke again. "They're invading... Father was out getting the mail from the postman and a German paratrooper came upon them..." Static. "He must've thought the postman was a soldier in his uniform... he shot and missed..."

"Is Father okay?" Betsy stammered, fearing the answer to come.

"He's dead, Betsy."

Their fears had come true. Germany had invaded the Netherlands. They'd promised to do so if the Dutch didn't surrender. The Dutch hadn't backed down, so they bombed Rotterdam. Thousands had died.

Paratroopers had landed and were getting to work. German soldiers were now on Dutch soil.

Jespar had said he'd never be able to live in an occupied Netherlands, and it seemed he wouldn't have to.

Betsy's heart broke.

The Netherlands surrendered, and as Rotterdam burned, everything changed. While the queen fled for safety, the people were left to deal with their invaders. In one fell swoop, what once had been their country felt yanked from their grasp.

At first many businesses and schools closed and, though they reopened, life was far from normal. German vehicles always seemed to be rolling down the streets. Men in uniform ate in restaurants, shopped in stores, and took over police departments.

Some Dutch families, like Femke's, were forced to give up their homes. The beautiful mansion, Slot Zeist, was to become a German headquarters. Others had their businesses integrated into German industry. The mill, the factories, and Betsy's father's company were all forced to comply.

"I don't want you walking alone," Hank told her one day.

Betsy nodded while washing some potatoes in the sink. She didn't want to think about any of this. They were to have Janet over for supper and she had just a few more preparations.

"You can take the car if you really need to leave the house," he said, "or else I'll pick up groceries for you."

"Is it really that dangerous?" Her voice quivered.

Hank shrugged. "Most of the soldiers are just like us... honest people who love their country. But some..." His voice trailed off. "I just don't want you in the wrong place at the wrong time."

Betsy nodded again. She felt safer at home anyway, but she also felt more alone with her thoughts. Her worries took on a life of their own in the confines of her four walls. A darkness that had risen up when her mother died seemed to have grown heavier and thicker.

Her sister arrived shortly and they sat down to eat, but tonight the delectable spread of roast chicken, biscuits, and steamed potatoes slathered in butter made Betsy's stomach churn. She hoped the others hadn't also lost their appetites.

"Arend says the company's being overrun," Janet said bluntly, cutting herself a piece of meat from the tray. "Father used to make the rules, but now everything's changed. They're forced to comply with demands, making ships for our enemies... does that seem fair?"

Betsy shook her head, quietly taking her husband's hand.

"I bet you're glad you left when you did." Janet flashed a look at Hank. "I bet you're feeling as free as a bird these days."

Though she'd never particularly favoured Hank, Janet seemed even colder towards him today.

Hank shook his head. "None of us will come out of this unscathed."

"Father worked all his life for this!" Janet threw up her hands. "He built something from nothing. He came from nothing, and now this is what happens? His company is forced to obey the enemy? Arend is up to his neck with work."

Heart racing, Betsy excused the boys.

Her sister was quiet for a moment. Then, turning to Betsy, she added, "Arend says we have no choice. He says we need to obey without question."

"Does the company really have a choice to do otherwise?" Hank asked quietly.

Betsy thought the question would further anger her sister, but instead Janet shrugged. "If we want to stay open... probably not."

Betsy swallowed. It *was* unfair. Though her sister could be headstrong, it was that very stubbornness that she loved.

Betsy didn't blame her for being angry.

Chapter Twelve

January 1941

"When will this let up?" Betsy whispered, massaging her temples, trying to ward off a headache.

She didn't have time for this today. Eliana had come to watch the children, and she had errands to run and groceries to get—flour, tea, onions, thread, soap, and a bit of pork if prices weren't too high.

Starting the ignition, she made her way down the street and towards the store. Though she had seen German vehicles around for months, she still wasn't used to the sight of them.

She arrived at the store, climbed out, and made her way inside. The grocer, Mr. Gerbrandy, bid her welcome as he stood filling the potato barrel. An empty carrot cart looked like it was next on the agenda.

As Betsy began gathering her needed items, she caught sight of her old friend Ada Veenstra. Standing beside her was a tall, strapping man in a German uniform. He carried Ada's basket and one of her little sons walked between the couple. They talked happily together, and Ada even slipped her hand inside the man's for a moment.

Swallowing hard, Betsy had a thousand questions.

Her friend spotted her and waved. She said something to the man and then made her way over to her, arms extended. Betsy tried to hide her shock.

"It's so good to see you!" Ada exclaimed.

"And you." Betsy attempted a smile. Why shouldn't she be glad to see her friend? Ada had been her old school pal, and they'd managed to keep up with each other into adulthood, though it appeared they had much to catch up about now.

The German picked up Ada's son and approached.

"I'd like to introduce to you Erich Schneider," Ada said, taking the man's arm.

The soldier nodded and smiled.

Betsy didn't know quite what to do. "Hello," she said weakly.

"I met Erich at a Christmas party," Ada explained, seeming to want Betsy's approval. She looked up at the man warmly and then tousled her son's hair. Betsy wondered if she'd ever seen her friend so animated. "He's been very kind and good with the children, you see. He takes the boys out for ice cream all the time, and he's even helped my mother with some vehicle repairs."

"I'm a mechanic," the man added. "Working on army vehicles is a breeze compared to working for my dad back home."

Though his accent was thick, Betsy could understand him well. He bounced the boy and made him laugh.

Ada seemed pleased, but Betsy still didn't know what to say. How could they act so casual, so at ease? Germany had invaded. That was the only reason Erich Schneider was in this country. How could they just pretend everything was okay?

At her silence, Erich offered to continue the shopping. Taking the boy, he made his way towards the produce while Ada stepped closer to speak.

"I know this may seem strange," Ada whispered. "I hate what's going on... and we're all afraid. But Erich is just a normal man. A good man, in fact."

Betsy nodded. Ada had lost her husband Pieter a year ago in a mill accident. Times had been hard for her, caring for two small boys and a widowed mother. Betsy had hoped the best for her, but was this it? Entertaining a German soldier whose country had invaded theirs?

Erich Schneider had no right courting sweet Ada, and he had no right to be here in the first place.

Even as Betsy said goodbye to her friend and made her way towards the onions, her heart felt convicted. Her mother had always said that bitterness stole one's joy. "Love your neighbours and your enemies," her mother would teach.

But what about in a war? What about when they were invading your home? Surely her mother wouldn't expect her to do that. Surely God wouldn't either.

April 1941

It was Sunday and Betsy was taking the children to church in the car. Oh how she missed the days when she could just push the carriage down the street and walk the few blocks in the sunshine. It was a warm day today, the perfect weather for a stroll.

But Hank thought it far too dangerous.

Betsy wished her husband would join her. She longed for the day when they'd all go together, not just on Christmas and Easter but every Sunday. Though the sermons were sometimes dry, she felt attending church was important. She wanted their children to know the Lord, and this was the best way she knew to encourage that.

She was happy Hank at least allowed them to go, but Sundays were when she felt the most distance between them. He'd help her get the children ready and clean up the breakfast dishes. When they headed out, he'd make his way to the workshop. Business was booming and he always had projects on the go.

The boys chatted happily as they drove, and when they arrived they filed into the service and found their usual place. Today the congregation was taking communion and Betsy looked forward to it. Eliana's words reverberated in her memory: *"When I'm sitting in church, I feel how much God loves me."*

"Let me feel that today, Father," Betsy whispered.

Reverend Vischer led them in singing hymns, and when the boys got fussy Janet offered to take them outside. Betsy had most of the songs memorized, but it was the last one that caught her attention:

O love of God, how rich and pure!
How measureless and strong![5]

---

[5] Frederick M. Lehman, "The Love of God," 1917.

Hands trembling as she held the tattered hymnal, Betsy wondered how many times she'd sung these words without thinking about what they meant. Sitting down on the hard pew, she marvelled at how many Sundays she'd done so out of habit, never really pausing to contemplate the love of Christ.

Reverend Vischer gave his sermon, but Betsy could hardly take her eyes off the little table at the front of the room. When the man finally got to it, she could hardly wait to partake.

"The Lord's body, broken for thee," he said.

Broken because of love.

Betsy pulled her sleeping daughter close. God's love was unmatched by any human on this earth. It was greater than her mother's love, though that had been precious. It was more than her sister's love, though hers was fierce. It was more than her children's love, though they loved her as much as they were able. It was even more than Hank's love, though his was passionate and steady.

It was a love that encompassed and then surpassed them all.

She ate the bread.

Reverend Vischer took the cup.

"The Lord's blood, shed for thee."

Tears streamed from her eyes. Her world was broken, and her heart had been too. The war had turned everything upside-down. Much had changed.

But one thing never would: the love of God. It was strong, measureless, and would never die. It was constant, though life ebbed and flowed. It was sure, whether she felt it or not.

And it made her weep.

September 1941

Betsy treasured every spare minute she spent alone. From bandaging cuts to breaking up squabbles, being a mother was a full-time job and then some.

But today she had some time to herself. John was at school, Henry played outside, and Elizabeth slept in the next room. So Betsy quietly made soup. Chopping the last carrot, she slid it into the steaming broth.

As she did, she heard a knock at the door. Turning from the pot, she wiped her hands on her apron and went to answer.

It was Eliana.

"This is a surprise." Betsy tilted her head. "You're not working today?"

As soon as she spoke, Betsy ascertained something in the girl's eyes. She was deeply troubled and Betsy welcomed her inside.

"Is everything okay?"

When Eliana met her gaze, Betsy saw that she was sweating.

"What is it, dear?" she asked, motherly concern in her voice. The girl was eighteen and Betsy had grown to care for her like a younger sister.

"I'm so scared," Eliana whispered.

The two sat down at the big oak table.

"My brother… is dead."

Betsy reached for the girl's hand. It was trembling. "I'm so sorry."

"The Germans… hate us."

Betsy knew that she meant the Jews. While she'd never seen it first-hand, she had heard of their cruelty, singling out Jewish people and regarding them as less than human.

"Samuel… he killed himself." Eliana could barely speak the words. She leaned over the table and covered her face with her hands.

Standing, Betsy went to the girl and put a hand on her shoulder. She stood beside the young woman for a long time, knowing what it was to grieve, but Eliana's grief was unique. Betsy would never be able to fully understand the pain and fear, and she didn't know how to help more.

"Samuel was a good brother," her friend whispered, her sobs subsiding. "He was younger than me, but he looked after me. He was very brave. And yet this all proved to be too much for him."

It's too much for everyone, Betsy wanted to say.

Elizabeth began to cry.

"Let me go to her," Eliana offered, seeming to want a distraction. Betsy nodded and the girl slipped from the room.

"What am I to do?" she prayed. She'd felt burdened for her friend before, but what she experienced now was different. She felt compassionate, protective, and heartbroken. Would the sadness ever end? Would the hardships ever stop?

How am I supposed to help her?

She knew she couldn't fix all these problems. Could she even fix one? She wanted to be useful, to make some small contribution to help alleviate the pain, but what could she do?

Returning to her soup, she gave it a stir. Smells of rosemary and sage made her mouth water. She knew that being there for Eliana meant a great deal. But something inside her felt there was more.

As Eliana returned with her daughter, Betsy opened the refrigerator and pulled out some cheese, ham, and bread.

"Will you join us for lunch?" she asked.

"I should actually be getting home to Mother," the girl replied.

When Eliana had gone, Betsy saw to Elizabeth's diaper and made some sandwiches, even as her husband came in from the shop.

As she worked, something shifted in her heart. While she couldn't fully explain it, she felt a keen sense deep down in her soul. There was more for her to do.

She felt the Lord speaking in a way she hadn't before. It was as if his still, small voice was whispering to her heart: *Wait. Be ready. I will show you what to do.*

Chapter Thirteen

December 1941

Betsy had never seen her husband so distracted. He sat at the table across from her, eating dinner and chatting with their sons. But she could tell something was different.

Winter had blown in. The temperatures were cooler and Betsy was diligent to keep the fire going in the hearth. She was thankful for a warm house to shield them from the cold, and she only wished it could shield them from the evil as well.

It'd been months since she'd felt the Lord speak to her heart, telling her to wait, telling her to be ready, that he would show her what to do.

So she had waited, but all had been silent. She'd asked Hank about it, to see if he had any ideas about what they could do for Eliana. But he had been less than helpful. In fact, he'd hardly seemed to hear her question.

At first, Betsy felt irritated. Why wasn't he talking to her? But as she prayed for wisdom, she continued to feel God's nudging to wait... wait for answers... wait for Hank.

Eyeing her husband now, she fed Elizabeth spoonfuls of stew and coaxed her sons to eat their vegetables. What was she seeing in his eyes?

"How was work?" she asked.

"It was good," he responded.

She waited for more, but there was nothing. He moved the potatoes, carrots, and meat with his fork but hardly took a bite.

Was he angry? No. Sad? It didn't appear so.

Curious, she helped the boys finish what was on their plates and wiped their mouths. Leaving the table, they went to play and Hank took Elizabeth from her so she could finish as well.

As she ate, she watched him. The toddler sat on his lap, gleefully laughing at his expressions and pulling his beard.

When the children were tucked in bed, the two of them set to work on dishes. A moment passed as they stood together in the tiny kitchen, Betsy at the sink and Hank drying the dishes. All was quiet, and Betsy prayed for guidance.

"How are you doing?" she asked.

"Good."

Sighing, Betsy rinsed a plate and tried again. "Were you able to finish Mr. Van Berg's clock?"

Hank just nodded and she thought she'd failed again. Waiting, she finished the last pan and drained the sink.

Suddenly, her husband spoke. "I had a good conversation with someone today. It got me thinking."

"Who was it? What were you thinking about?" Betsy couldn't contain her questions.

"Old Mr. Haze… told me about what he's been reading."

"A book?"

"A pamphlet. Lots of them."

Confused, Betsy waited for more.

"He gave me some and I started reading them at lunch."

"What are they about?" she asked.

"Everything," he answered vaguely. "The world. Germans. Jews." He paused. "God."

Betsy's heart skipped a beat, but she hardly knew why. Her husband had heard about God all his life. What was so different about these pamphlets? What had they said, and what did her husband think of them?

Hank didn't speak for a time. He finished drying the dishes and put them away quietly, so as not to disturb the children. Ushering her to the sofa, he put his arms around her. She leaned her head on his chest and waited, praying. Something was happening. She didn't know what, but she didn't want to spoil it.

January 1942

Her husband hadn't shared more or tried to explain about the pamphlets, but Betsy watched him. For weeks he'd come in from work, eat dinner, put the children to bed, and read. She wanted to read the pamphlets herself, but it all felt too sacred. She wanted to ask more questions, but would it ruin the miracle she foresaw?

One day, he did speak. She had just put Elizabeth down for the night and wanted to sleep herself, but the look in her husband's eyes quickly dissuaded her.

"Can we talk?" he asked, taking her hand.

Nodding, she followed him to the big oak table and sat down. Anxious, excited, and uncertain, she waited.

Hank didn't speak for a moment, but when he did he took both her hands and looked her straight in the eye. "I've been reading a lot, Betsy."

Betsy smiled. "I know."

"And you've graciously asked no questions."

She had wanted to.

"I've spent weeks poring over these pamphlets." He handed her one from his pocket. "Reverend Slomp's words have resonated with me. He sees God in a way I never have before." Stopping, he seemed uncertain with his words. "Growing up, faith was empty. It was just a bunch of rules…"

Betsy's grasp tightened. She'd sometimes felt that way too. She'd struggled to see God as anything but harsh and demanding. But now she saw him differently, rightly. She'd experienced his love.

"Reverend Slomp wrote about how God saves us," he continued. "I guess I always thought it was up to me."

"What else does he say?" She leaned closer.

"He says we need to love others. We need to help them."

Betsy tilted her head. "You're always kind, Hank. You've helped a lot of people in this town. Remember how you repaired Ada's radio and fixed Diederik's roof?"

Her husband nodded. "Reverend Slomp says we need to help the Jews. Jesus was a Jew, you know. They're God's people."

Betsy searched her husband's blue eyes, thinking of sweet Eliana and her burden for the girl. Was this God's answer to her prayer?

"Things are getting bad, dangerous even. God's people are being sent off... put in camps."

"What are we supposed to do?"

"Help them." Her husband's reply was quick. It was as if he'd already determined his course, and it was simple.

She just wanted to know more.

"I'm nervous, Hank." Betsy squeezed his hands in hers. "How are we supposed to help them?"

He shook his head. "I don't fully know. People need to stay informed. Jews need to stay informed."

Betsy nodded. Her husband kissed her hands and then wrapped her in his arms.

"Betsy, I think I'm starting to see God as he really is. Does that make sense?"

"Tell me more," she coaxed.

"I used to see him as irritable and small and waiting with a big stick in his hand... wondering if I'd mess up. And I've messed up a lot."

"How do you see him now?"

He smelled of sawdust and lemon soap. "I am beginning to see him as kind... big enough to save me from my sins... giving me a purpose that makes my heart come alive."

"Are you afraid?"

"I suppose so."

Betsy felt uneasy too. There were so many uncertainties, and yet she felt her fears melting away as she looked up at the man who held her. Hank was at peace. God had met him, and they would be okay.

Chapter Fourteen

May 1942

Months passed and Hank didn't mention the pamphlets again. Betsy wondered and prayed and watched. Her husband had changed. That much was clear. But how he felt God was leading them to care for Jews, she didn't know.

In May, their world changed again. Every Jew was required to wear a badge bearing the star of David. This would identify them—put a target on their backs, as it were. Eliana had showed up to work wearing hers. The boys, unaware of its meaning, thought it splendid, but Betsy shuddered at the sight. Now everyone would know. They would know Eliana's heritage. They would know her faith. And they would know she was banned from cafes, parks, riding streetcars, and even riding her bike.

It was no longer safe for her to take the children out. Betsy would do the grocery shopping and the children would stay home with their nanny.

Thankfully Eliana had agreed to stay a bit later today. Though Betsy only had a few items on her list, she would stop by Janet's on her way home. She and her sisters were having their weekly coffee time and she hated to miss it.

Pulling into Janet's drive, she unloaded her bags and let herself in. Her childhood home never changed, and it was a comfort. The same bench still sat in the entry, the same sofa still graced the living room, and the familiar family pictures still hung on the wall. In a world that was constantly in flux, the Baer family home seemed immutable.

Angela and Hannie sat together on the sofa, poring over women's fashion magazines.

As Betsy entered, Angela looked up and smiled. "Someone's been shopping!"

Betsy grinned and set down her groceries, hoping to keep some things cool during their visit.

Hannie piped up as she usually did. "*I've* been shopping!"

Betsy laughed and scurried into the kitchen where her older sister was pulling cookies out of the oven.

"Mother would be abhorred by this spread," Janet remarked. "Cookies, cake, and buttery rolls."

"And not a piece of fruit in sight," Betsy added, slipping her package of beef and carton of eggs into the refrigerator.

Though joking, there was a seriousness beneath their words. Their mother had battled cancer for years and eaten diligently to try and fight it. She had always told her daughters to be careful, fearing they were prone to the illness too. Thankfully, no one else had been diagnosed, though Betsy had been feeling sick more often these days. Headaches and fatigue were frequent. While she'd never gone to a doctor for them, she was beginning to wonder if she might need to.

"Help me bring these trays out," Janet instructed, forever the older sister.

Betsy did as she was told, forever the younger.

They filled the dining room table with Janet's delicacies, then all took their places—Janet at the head, Betsy beside, and the other two girls across from them. Hannie's new baby sat in his highchair at the end.

Hannie was only now finishing her tale. "I got three new blouses, a new pair of heels, and a hat that looks divine."

"I'm surprised Isaak lets you buy as much as you do," Janet commented, pouring herself some coffee.

Hannie made a face. "My husband doesn't boss me around," she said with a laugh.

"And I don't think he's scraping for money," Angela added with a wink.

"He's loving his government job!" Hannie replied.

Janet sighed. "I'm more surprised you can spend your time shopping at all when the world is so chaotic."

"The Germans don't dictate my spending habits," Hannie retorted. "They can do what they want with the Jews for all I care… take them all off the streetcars and ban them from public places. It's not my business. In fact, life has been pretty good since they arrived."

Betsy swallowed hard.

"Hannie! You're heartless," Angela declared.

"Call me what you will. I don't intend to risk my life and my family to help them."

Angela frowned. "And what if *they* were your family?"

"Well, they're not." Hannie giggled, running her fingers through her lovely locks.

Baby Frans began to fuss, and Hannie looked at Janet helplessly. Sighing loud enough for everyone to hear, Janet stood and took the baby from his seat.

Betsy turned to Angela. "How is the company doing?"

"It's exhausting." Angela cut herself a slice of cake. "Every day, Arend comes home weary and frustrated. It seems he can barely keep up with *their* demands."

"Oh, please, let's talk no more of war!" Hannie sighed. "It's not as bad as people say. The Germans have even offered Isaak…"

Her voice trailed off, seeming to catch herself.

Betsy's ears perked up, but she feared asking more. She too felt laden with secrets. What would her sisters think if she told them what Hank had said all those months ago?

September 1942

Her head hurt, throbbing this time. Betsy was used to the ache. She'd sit down, drink water, and wait for it to pass. But this was different. Her eyes felt strained and her vision blurred ever so slightly. She sat on the sofa while Elizabeth played at her feet.

The two boys were at school today, little Henry having recently joined his brother. Elizabeth was thankfully content, playing with her dolls and chattering away. The girl loved make-believe, and she was learning how to entertain herself, though it'd been an adjustment not having her brother around.

Betsy smiled at her daughter, but another sharp pain pricked her like so many needles. She covered her face with her hands and closed her eyes, willing the pain away but having no success.

Perhaps a cool cloth would help.

"Stay here, Elizabeth," she whispered. "Mama will be right back."

Running to the kitchen sink, she immersed a rag, wrung it, and pressed it to her brow. She poured herself a glass of water and lay down on the sofa.

"Mama, look!" Elizabeth squealed, standing to her feet and nestling close, holding her baby out for inspection.

"What a pretty dress," Betsy complimented, tugging on the doll's blue frock.

Elizabeth, forever a sweetheart, grinned and kissed it.

Betsy smiled... then there was more throbbing. Harder, faster this time. She turned the cloth and clenched her jaw.

A serious expression crossed the girl's face. "Mama sick," she said perceptively.

"Mama's okay. I just need to rest."

"Baby sick too!" the girl declared, laying the doll beside her.

Betsy smiled. "Go put Baby to bed."

Elizabeth took the doll in her arms, hugged it, then flung it on the floor, distracted by her brother's blocks. Teetering away, the sweet girl talked happily to herself.

Betsy was thankful for her distraction. She wished she could be so easily diverted from the pain.

Chapter Fifteen

November 1942

The air was warm with spices. A pot of stew sat bubbling on the stove, the lid clinking quietly. It was a wonder it didn't boil over for how distracted Betsy felt. Her husband seemed restless, even more than usual. He'd come in early from the shop, washed, helped her prepare dinner, and now sat playing with the children. He'd been unusually quiet and Betsy had tried hopelessly to ascertain what was on his mind. Turning now to the table, she saw that he'd set out two extra plates.

"Are we having company?" she asked.

"Yes," her husband replied from the sofa, not looking up.

Betsy stared at him, questions filling her mind. Why hadn't he told her sooner?

As expected, a sudden bubbling came from the stove. Spinning on her heel, Betsy grabbed the overflowing pot.

"Ouch!" she cried.

Hank was quickly by her side with a towel. "Are you okay?" he asked, taking the pot from her hands.

She nodded even as her rosy hand burned.

Hank turned on the faucet and motioned her over. "Let it run under cold water," he quietly instructed.

Betsy was embarrassed. Her mind had been elsewhere, but her questions still weren't answered.

"Daddy, come play!" Henry hollered.

"Are you sure you're all right?" Her husband put a hand on her shoulder.

Betsy nodded. She hated her husband's secrets, but his faith seemed stronger than ever. His was not a dry, empty religion. It seemed anything but. He didn't always attend church with her and sometimes a curse word slipped from his lips—habits were hard to break—but the fire in his eyes, his thirst for God's Word, even his love for her, burned brighter than ever. For all that, she was thankful. She wouldn't worry over the other things. God would mould Hank Vischer, and she would stay quiet until led to do otherwise.

She was just about to call her family for supper when a knock sounded on the door. Hank bolted from the floor, where his children surrounded him. He turned and looked at her ever so quickly, and in that brief moment Betsy glimpsed something new. It wasn't just passion; it was commitment, something steady and full of faith.

She took a deep breath, trusting him, trusting God. Whatever was behind that door, she knew they would be okay.

Without saying a word, Hank turned the squeaky knob and ushered in two gentlemen, dressed warmer than necessary for the weather. Though it was a mild September night, they were so bundled that she could hardly make out their faces.

"Welcome." Hank greeted them, as though he knew them already. Betsy had no clue who they were.

Henry and Elizabeth curiously eyed the strangers while shy John ran to his mother. Betsy also felt shy. Her heart pounded, ascertaining that this was no ordinary social call.

"Let me take your coats," Hank offered. The two men removed their wraps, and then Hank turned to her once more. "This is my wife, Betsy."

The strangers nodded. One was tall and slender, a Dutch man through and through. The other, a fair amount older, stood slightly hunched over with an unkept beard, shaggy hair, and kind eyes.

"Would you mind closing the curtains, Hank?" the older gentleman asked, a note of familiarity in his voice.

How did he know Hank? Was he a businessman like her husband?

As Hank went to shade the windows, Betsy swallowed hard. Secrecy. Though she'd wondered when things might change, she longed to hold onto the feelings of normalcy in her home. The world could shift, but she loved closing her door, caring for her children, and pretending everything was as it should be.

Now it seemed the world had come through her door. The world was with her children. The pain and brokenness felt too close for comfort.

"Are you hungry?" Hank asked the men.

"Let's talk first," the older gentleman replied. The young, taller man hadn't said a word. He just followed Hank and the other to the sofa.

Hank turned to his wife. "Would you mind sending the children out?"

Betsy nodded absentmindedly. Pulling Elizabeth into her arms, she called for the boys to follow. John came willingly, but Henry took more convincing.

When they were all in the boys' room, John looked at her. "Who are those men, Mama?"

Betsy shook her head. "I don't know, son. Can you watch your little brother and sister?"

John nodded.

"I don't need watching!" Henry declared. "I'm five!"

Betsy smiled and tousled the boy's blond curls. "Then you both watch Elizabeth."

Her daughter was already paging through her brothers' books. She wasn't usually allowed to do so.

"Not that one!" Henry almost shrieked, running to his sister's side.

"*You* read to her," Betsy prompted.

Eyes gleaming, the boy stood a little taller. "*I'll* read to you!" he shouted, as if it was his own brilliant idea.

Though she longed to stay with her children, Betsy turned to go. She knew her husband would want her by his side.

As she made her way into the living room, she lifted her worries to God. *I don't know what's happening, Lord. Give me strength.*

The darkness inside was thickening. While she could usually keep the sadness and anxiety at bay, today they felt a little stronger, a little louder.

Betsy stopped in her tracks. She didn't want to move. She wanted to run away, or perhaps just curl up in a ball and close her eyes. She wanted to shut out the world.

"Help!" was all she could whisper.

Then, as if right on cue, Betsy heard the familiar piano music from the house next door. Diederik was at it again.

The soul that on Jesus doth lean for repose,
I will not, I will not, desert to his foes;
That soul, though all hell should endeavor to shake,
I'll never, no never, no never forsake.

"Do you know why these men are here, Betsy?" Hank's voice was soft, gentle with her and quiet enough for the children not to hear.

Betsy shook her head. How *could* she know? Sitting with her husband on the threadbare sofa, she felt totally lost to what was going on. She didn't know who these strangers were, just like she didn't know what her husband had been up to for so many months. She only knew that things were changing and she must trust the Lord with whatever transpired.

Hank took both her hands and looked in her eyes, as if they were the only two in the room.

"I believe God is leading our path, Betsy. I believe this is his will, and I know he will protect us."

Taking a shaky breath, Betsy squeezed his hands. She knew that too, and yet she hated needing protection. She wished they could just avoid danger entirely.

"I'll never, no never, no never forsake."

The older gentleman spoke next, his voice husky yet warm. "My name is Reverend Fritz Slomp."

Betsy straightened, recognizing his name. Hank had read his pamphlets a hundred times over. The man's words had spoken to her husband in a miraculous way. Now he was sitting on her sofa. This must be important.

The man continued. "Have you ever heard of Mrs. Kuipers-Rietberg?"

Betsy shook her head, and her husband leaned close. "She's the leader of the resistance."

Resistance... those who stood up to Germany... those who said no... those who risked their lives to do what they thought was right.

Betsy shivered.

The elderly man pressed on. "She has appointed me leader of the underground."

"What does that mean?" she asked.

"Many people's lives are in danger, Mrs. Vischer."

She nodded. "You mean the Jews."

"Yes, but not only them. The Dutch, Germans... anyone who resists. Things are getting so bad. People need hiding."

"Underground?"

Reverend Slomp nodded. "That's where I come in. I need to find hiding places for these people." He turned and looked at the young gentleman beside him. "That's where this man comes in. He needs a place to stay." Then he looked back at Betsy. "And that's where you come in..."

Betsy swallowed. She didn't want him to continue. She didn't want to hear him ask. She knew what he was saying, at least in part, and it was enough to make her afraid. Hiding people? Such a task would be fraught with danger... not only for Hank and her, but for their children. This was their home, and now it was being invaded.

She clenched her eyes shut, willing herself to breathe. Her heart started pounding and she felt the world closing in again.

"Betsy?" Hank's voice broke through the shadows. He'd seen her have minor panic attacks before. Taking her by the arms, they stood. "Open your eyes, Betsy," he whispered.

She did as she was told. Scanning the room, she tried to collect herself—inhale, exhale, inhale, exhale.

Their visitors were quiet and Betsy was embarrassed, but finally her breathing slowed. Hank patiently stood beside her.

Suddenly, she heard Elizabeth crying in the other room.

"I must go to her," Betsy said, thankful for an escape but knowing it wouldn't change the reality of their situation.

She went to her daughter.

"I'm hungry!" Henry moaned.

"I know, son." Betsy tried to smile. Their supper was surely cold.

"Who are those men, Mama?" John asked again.

"Daddy's friends." It was all Betsy could muster.

She soothed her daughter and grabbed a few pieces of bread for her sons, not caring whether it spoiled their dinner. When she returned, her daughter in her arms, the older man stood to go. The younger one lingered.

"I'm afraid I must leave," Reverend Slomp said, turning to face her. "Do you read Scripture, Mrs. Vischer?"

She replied truthfully. "Not as much as I should."

The man waved her comment away as he slipped on his coat. "It's my lifeline. In it, the Lord Jesus reminds me that he will never leave me or forsake me. I find peace in that."

Betsy nodded. She did too. She looked at the young man and then at her husband. Hank stared at her intently, taking her free hand.

"Are you with me, Betsy?" he asked, his question holding a double meaning they both ascertained.

She nodded. She was with him, fearful yet committed to doing what the Lord called them to do.

When Reverend Slomp left, she turned to the young gentleman. Having no idea where he would hide, what their days would now look like, or how things would have to change, she asked, "Would you join us for dinner?"

Chapter Sixteen

The man's name was Sem Van Dyke. He looked about thirty years old and he'd joined the resistance movement a few months ago. However, he'd quickly been discovered and was no longer safe.

They all sat down to dinner. Hank prayed and the children began complaining about eating their vegetables. It was as if nothing had changed, though everything had.

"Are you from Zeist?" Betsy asked their visitor, scooping some potatoes onto his plate.

"I grew up in Amsterdam," he replied coldly. "Moved to Utrecht five years ago."

Betsy had a hundred questions. Did he have a wife? Children? What did they think of his work? What exactly had he done for the resistance?

Henry asked the next question, trying to figure out why they had a stranger at their table. "Are you running away from home?" he said through a mouthful of stew meat.

"Henry," Betsy reprimanded. His manners needed work on all fronts.

"No." Sem shook his head. He was neither offended nor especially friendly with the boy. Betsy didn't know how to read him. "My home is anywhere I lay my head."

"Where are your parents?" her son persisted. "Do you have kids?"

Betsy tried to quell his inquiries, but the boy ignored her gestures.

"My parents died a long time ago, and my wife wants nothing to do with me. That means I don't see my children either."

Henry finally got right to it. "Why are you here?"

"Hush…" Betsy touched his arm.

"It's all right, Betsy," her husband said. "The children ought to know something."

Betsy grew quiet. Still unable to wrap her mind around the whole thing, she would leave her husband to handle this.

"Mr. Van Dyke will be staying with us for a while." Her husband looked at their sons. "But it's a secret. You know what a secret is, right?"

John didn't respond, often letting his younger brother do the talking, a task which Henry was happy to perform.

"A secret's when you don't tell!" Henry crowed.

Her husband nodded. "That's right. We mustn't tell anyone that Mr. Van Dyke is here."

Henry wrinkled his brow. "Why not?"

Hank was quiet, scratching his beard and contemplating his words. "Think of it like a game. Tell someone, and you're out."

Though her husband was speaking in jest, Betsy discerned the terrible truth beneath his words. If anyone found out that Sem was there, they might very well be out, taken away to who knew where.

John and Henry seemed content with their father's explanation, but Hank pressed the matter.

"Not a word, Henry," Hank said.

John wouldn't be a problem. It was his little brother who liked to talk.

Henry saw his father's seriousness and crossed his arms. "What about Dirk or Sven?"

"None of your friends."

Henry wasn't done, but he put a large spoonful of potato in his mouth anyway. "What about Van or Ferdi?"

"None of your cousins."

"Don't talk with your mouth full," Betsy murmured out of habit.

Henry chewed over his father's words as he took another bite of supper.

Betsy knew she mustn't tell anyone either—not her sisters, or Eliana, or Diederik. Janet would be the hardest; they'd never been able to keep secrets from each other.

Guard my lips.

When they'd finished eating, Sem helped them clear the table and then played with the boys in the living room.

Betsy turned to her husband. "What do you know of him?"

"I know he's a resistance fighter," Hank replied matter-of-factly.

"Is he a man of faith?"

Hank smiled, taking her by the shoulders. "People get involved for all sorts of reasons, my angel. I'm guessing his were political." Seeing her anxiety, he leaned close and kissed her forehead. "I know he's a hard worker. Reverend Slomp thinks highly of him, and we'll pray for him. I think he'll come around."

Betsy nodded, trusting her husband's discernment.

"Where will he stay?" she asked, looking about the room. They had two bedrooms, one for the boys and one for them and Elizabeth. They hadn't much of an attic and little space anywhere else.

Hank pointed to the trapdoor in the pantry. It led to their cellar where Betsy stored canned vegetables and jam.

"Won't that be too obvious?" she asked.

"We'll remove the door and add another more discreet one," her husband said, as if he'd long been contemplating his course. "I'll get to work on it right away."

With that, he headed out to the workshop and Betsy finished wiping the counters. Opening the refrigerator, she scanned the contents. A small block of cheese, a little bread, and some leftover beef. Though they had vegetables for months, she feared it wouldn't be enough to feed another.

Provide for us.

As she put the boys to bed that night, they peppered her with questions.

"How long will Sem stay here?" Henry asked, climbing in beside his brother.

Betsy sat beside them and prayed for the words to say. "Call him Mr. Van Dyke. And I'm afraid I don't know."

"Is Mr. Van Dyke sad?" John implored, pulling the quilt up to his chin. He hadn't spoken at all at supper, but now he looked worried.

Betsy took his hand. Oh how he reminded her of herself. "It seems that way," she whispered.

"How can we make him feel better?" John asked next.

Betsy shook her head, unsure how to answer.

"Should we pray for him?" Henry shot up from his pillow, ready to get to work.

Betsy smiled. "That's a great idea."

Once all the children were tucked in, Betsy made her way back to the kitchen. Sem had found a book to read and Hank returned promptly from the shop.

"You'll sleep in the cellar tonight," Hank told the man. "And tomorrow we'll finish constructing the new door."

Betsy wanted to know where he'd put said door, and he seemed to read her mind.

With a twinkle in his eye, Hank declared, "Right beneath the table."

♪♫♪

Hank made quick work, and by the next evening he'd built a new trapdoor and had the old one completely boarded up. Betsy gave their visitor, if he could be called that, a basket of cheese and apples. Hank brought him a lamp and blanket and the three of them stood together on the cold floor. All was dark except the light from the door above.

"Help yourself to whatever you need, should we not be able to bring you dinner," Hank said,

He pointed to the extra vegetables and preserves in the corner. Sacks of onions and potatoes were wedged against the wall and jars of pickled carrots, apple jelly, and beans lined the solitary shelf and some overturned crates.

Then he indicated the wooden containers. "Store your things under there should you need to disappear."

Shuddering, Betsy knew their house may well be searched. What if someone discovered the trapdoor hidden under their table? Betsy prayed it wouldn't come to that.

Sem crossed his arms, seeming sceptical of Hank's plan. "And what if I have to hide further?"

Betsy grew tense. He didn't trust them, but why should he? She struggled to trust *him* as well.

Hank looked at Betsy, seeking her wisdom. Betsy only had to think a moment.

"The tarp," she whispered. "In your workshop."

Hank had a few tarps and old pieces of furniture out back. They could move a few underground and create a sort of camouflage. It may not work, but it was the best they could do.

"And how am I to know what's happening?" Sem questioned.

For the first time, Betsy saw beneath his hard exterior. He was terrified.

Hank put his hand on the man's shoulder. "We'll alert you if needed. Don't be afraid. The Lord is with you."

Betsy's heart swelled. God had worked powerfully in Hank Vischer's life. It was a miracle, and for a moment joy overshadowed all fear.

"I struggle to believe that God cares about any of this," Sem admitted. His coldness toward the things of God was obvious.

Draw him to you.

They bid Sem goodnight and headed upstairs. Since the children were in bed, she and Hank had some time alone. Sitting together on the sofa, Hank pulled her close and nuzzled his face in her hair.

"Did I say the right thing, Betsy?" he whispered.

Betsy looked at him in surprise. "Of course you did. Why do you ask?"

"Sem is... who I used to be..."

She understood his meaning. "But you've changed."

"God answered your prayers. He changed me by showing me who he is."

She rested her hand on his strong chest, rejoicing in God's grace. The steady beat of his heart never failed to calm her own. He had always been a good husband and father, but now he was a godly one. Now he was at peace.

"I want God to change Sem like he changed me," Hank confessed, rising and putting another log on the fire.

"He can," Betsy promised. She had seen firsthand what God could do in someone's heart.

Returning to his seat, Hank chuckled. "I'll never understand why you chose me, Betsy. You could've done so much better."

Betsy smiled. "I made an excellent choice, Hank Vischer. I chose the handsomest of them all."

He feigned offence. "So you just like me for my looks?"

"You also make me laugh."

"So just my humour?"

Grinning, Betsy swatted him, then wrapped her arms around his neck, looking him straight in the eye. "I chose you because you're the kindest, strongest, and wisest man I know."

Hank kissed her again. "And you're an angel."

Chapter Seventeen

December 1942

Another Christmas Day was upon them and Betsy prayed for the strength to get through the holidays, for she'd been sick a lot recently. Some days she'd be laid up in bed for hours. Her head would ache and she'd feel nauseous and exhausted.

While they'd managed to keep Sem's presence a secret, her illness felt more conspicuous. A few weeks ago, she'd found a lump on her right breast. Hank had tried to get her to go to the doctor, but she'd insisted it would go away on its own.

Deep inside, however, she feared the worst—a diagnosis that would change their lives like it had for her mother… like it had for little Betsy all those years ago.

Please, Lord. Not that.

As she helped Janet hang a few last decorations later that day, she turned to her sister. "If anything were to happen to me, Janet… please take care of the children. Help Hank—"

"Nonsense, little sister," Janet interrupted. Picking up a bowl of stuffing, she took Betsy's arm. "You're probably just tired."

She only called her *little sister* when she wanted to boss her around. Betsy crumpled on Janet's shoulder, trying not to cry. Though her sister wasn't affectionate, she was compassionate, and beneath the hard exterior there was a warm heart that only few got to see. Betsy was one of the lucky ones.

"Hush now," Janet whispered, hearing a few people approach from the dining room. She looked Betsy in the eye. "I'll always be here."

She pinned Betsy with her gaze, and for a split second both women stood motionless, as if willing time to stand still, wishing they could shield one another from all future pain and loss.

"And you will be here too," Janet added, as if needing to assure them both of something beyond their control.

Betsy smiled. "Thank you."

They made their way to the table and Hank came up beside her. Betsy took his hand, never tiring of his nearness, always enchanted by his warmth.

"Mama!" Elizabeth was at her knees, arms outstretched, imploring to be held.

"Yes, darling." Betsy scooped her up. The girl was getting big now, running and laughing with her brothers, but she'd always return to her mother, needing to be held every once in a while before getting back at it. "Where are your brothers?"

"Upstairs," Elizabeth replied.

The boys loved playing with Uncle Arend's old trains.

Her daughter had probably tried to join in, but often her pudgy hands made a mess of their games, much to her brothers' chagrin.

Betsy squeezed her daughter, taking in her sweet scent. Her cheeks were soft and warm, her hands clasping Betsy's face and ears and hair.

"Dinner is served!" Janet soon announced.

As she expected, her boys were down in a flash.

Everyone sat down. Arend said the blessing and they all partook. The room bustled with life. The big grandfather clock chimed five. The enticing aromas of turkey, ham, and pies made her mouth water.

Betsy loved being with her family, and so far no one had discovered the truth—that they were hiding someone in their cellar. It felt strange to keep such a secret, but she knew it was necessary. She only prayed for Sem's safety, not only because she cared for him but because their safety was so entangled with his. If he were caught, they would be too.

Let it not be so, Lord.

"Are you all right?" Hank touched her elbow.

Betsy smiled. "Of course."

They finished filling their children's plates and then served their own. Betsy's stomach growled.

"How's work going, Hank?" Arend asked, taking a bite of stuffing.

"It's going good," he replied. "Lots of radios to fix."

Again, another secret. While it was true that Hank was busy fixing radios, he spent most of his time doing other things. His involvement in the resistance extended much further than hiding Sem. Betsy didn't even know what all he did. Reverend Slomp was in regular communication with him, and he made good use of Hank's abilities.

"Like you always say, people need to stay informed," Arend said with a chuckle. He always seemed to have a smile on his face.

Hannie, however, was quick to chime in. "We all hope this blasted war ends soon. If Dutch people weren't so stubborn, we could all work together. Their resistance will be the end of us."

From under the table, Betsy took her husband's hand.

"You forget, Hannie," Angela said. "You're just as Dutch as the rest of us."

"But *I'm* not hiding Jews," Hannie retorted angrily. She turned to her husband, Isaak, who sat quietly beside her. "Isaak was offered some money to—"

Touching her shoulder, her husband stopped her. Everyone felt the tension rising. It was no secret where Isaak and Hannie stood politically.

Betsy heard Janet's fork clank, and she wondered how her sister would react. Would she blow up or storm out? Betsy waited… but there was nothing. She didn't know whether to worry or rejoice. Janet simply listened, not looking up, not saying a word. But in her eyes, Betsy could see the heaviness.

Arend quickly smiled. "We're happy that work is going well for you, Hank."

Trying to avoid making eye contact with anyone, Betsy instead gazed at her children, hoping they needed her; they were happily eating Janet's cooking, as content as ever.

"At least resistance fighters are doing something to help the Jews," Janet murmured.

"Janet, the Jews have proved to be nothing but trouble," Hannie interjected. "What loyalty do we have to them?"

"Let's talk of something else," Arend voted, seeing the mixed reactions. It was Christmas, after all.

Betsy stole a glance at her husband, wondering what he was thinking, but Hank's expression betrayed nothing. He busily partook of Janet's turkey and then helped himself to seconds.

When the meal was done, Betsy felt tired. She wanted to help with dishes, but Janet commanded her to rest.

"I'll not see you lifting a finger," she told her.

Janet's kindness was always serious and to-the-point, but Betsy felt the love in her words. She always looked out for her.

Climbing the old staircase, she went to rest in Janet's room, where she had used to sleep as a child. The papered walls, big window, and pretty curtains brought back a hundred memories. The two girls used to talk late into the night, whispering so no one would hear. Even when they were older, both unmarried for a few years, they had spent hours talking, laughing or crying. They'd shared everything.

If Betsy could tell anyone about Sem, she'd want it to be Janet. This was perhaps the first secret she had ever kept from her sister.

Lying down, she stared up at the rafters, willing the headache to pass, but it only got worse.

"Lord," she began, "I wish I could tell someone. These secrets feel too heavy to bear."

And with that she closed her eyes and drifted off to sleep.

Chapter Eighteen

"Bram, this is a surprise!" Though her brother-in-law was bundled from head to foot, Betsy could still make out his familiar grin.

"Mother sent me over with some leftover *Kerstkransjes* cookies!" Bram said. "Perhaps the children would like to help put them on the tree."

Betsy smiled. They hadn't seen Hank's parents that Christmas. Hank was more at odds with his parents than ever, as he and his father had had a heated debate last time they were over. Hank had offhandedly remarked that the Germans had no right to invade and needed to be stopped. His father had said to turn the other cheek.

Hank had surprised them all by asking questions. "And pervert justice? And let innocent people be killed?"

Everyone had fallen silent and Hank's parents had informed them it'd be better if they didn't come for Christmas that year. They had complied, but that meant not seeing Bram either.

Now, as he stood in her living room, Betsy was confused.

"I feel torn, Betsy," Bram said, slipping out of his coat.

Betsy was thankful she had just boiled the kettle, and she scooped some tea leaves into a waiting pot.

Had Bram sneaked out to come here? She wasn't sure she should ask.

Her brother-in-law quietly sat in an armchair and Betsy retrieved two cups and saucers. When the tea was steeped, she served them both and plunked down on the sofa. Hank and the children were out sledding and would be coming in shortly, but Bram seemed to want a private conversation anyway.

"I think Hank is right," Bram mumbled. "God wants us to do justice. My seminary professors often talked about that."

Betsy nodded and sat down. Bram hadn't been able to keep up with his studies and was apparently taking some time off.

He continued. "And yet aren't we supposed to love our enemies? Father says this world is not our home, and we mustn't fight back."

Betsy took a sip of her tea. Her body ached, and now her head did too.

"I don't know the answer, Bram," she replied truthfully. Hadn't Bram always been the smart one? If anyone had an answer, wouldn't he?

"I was also thinking..." Bram bit his nail and took a sip. "If I were to hide people in my home, would I ever be able to lie about it? Could I sin in order to protect an innocent person?"

At this, Betsy's heart dropped. "Those are... hard questions."

"I want to find the answers..." Bram smiled but seemed distracted, listless.

Suddenly the door opened and the children rushed in, bringing a cold wind with them. Hank was on their heels.

"Uncle Bram!" John exclaimed.

"Did you bring us presents?" Henry asked, throwing his coat on the floor and rushing over.

Betsy resisted the urge to reprimand him.

"I see you didn't bring your girlfriend along," her husband joked.

Bram blushed. "You mean Fenna?"

"Do you have more than one?"

Betsy stood to gather up coats, but her muscles protested. Not wanting to make a scene, she sat down again.

"Fenna and I are done," Bram insisted.

"Why is that?" she pried.

"I don't know. Father never liked her... and she... I didn't feel..."

Betsy had never seen him like this. Hank sat beside his wife while the children dove into the cookies. Bram had never been totally sure of himself, and he'd always turned to others for validation. But he seemed even weaker today. All peace seemed to have vanished.

"I best be going." Bram rose. "I don't want Mother to know…"

"Send her our love," Betsy said out of habit. Mrs. Vischer would probably never know of this visit.

Bram slipped on his coat and the children thanked him for the cookies.

When he was gone, the children, having more sledding to do, bundled up again and headed out.

Hank helped Betsy put potatoes in to roast for supper. "What did you make of that?" he asked, turning to her.

She knew he was referring to Bram's visit and shook her head. "I don't know. He seemed… anxious."

Her husband nodded, pulling out some beans from the refrigerator. "Unpredictable."

Betsy nodded as she set plates on the table. Bram's questions were understandable, and yet she knew he couldn't be trusted. He didn't know about Sem—about their involvement with the resistance.

And he never could.

January 1943

"Where has she gone?" Betsy beseeched her elderly neighbour.

Eliana had given her note of resignation three days ago with not a word or reason why. Betsy had gone to see Diederik about it, and he told her that she'd resigned there as well.

The old man shook his head. "I don't know where she is, young lady," he confessed.

A chilly wind nipped at their ears and Diederik quickly ushered her inside. Everywhere Betsy looked, things were in disarray. Papers, books, and dishes sat on every surface and the floor desperately needed a sweep.

"I've been worried about that girl ever since Samuel passed," Diederik said, shaking his head.

Betsy nodded. Eliana and her brother had been very close. When he'd died, something had died in her as well. But it wasn't just Samuel's death that made Betsy anxious. Eliana's whole family was in danger too. She prayed they were safe, and she feared they were not.

Diederik cleared a chair and invited Betsy to sit. He then got them some orange juice.

"Do you know why she quit?" Betsy asked, running her finger over the glass's smooth rim.

"Not exactly." The old man dropped his gaze. "But I don't doubt it's to do with what's going on. She's not safe, and she knows it. I wish I had done more for that girl. I don't even know where she lives to check in on her."

Betsy realized she didn't know either. She'd offered to drive her home many times, but Eliana had always refused. Had she simply not trusted her? Was that also why she was breaking ties now?

Betsy dropped her head. At least when Eliana worked for them, she could watch out for her. She hated not knowing what was going on.

Looking around the room, Betsy noticed that the piano cover had been removed and a hymnal sat open.

"Have you been playing today? I've been out grocery shopping and fear I've missed it."

Diederik smiled sadly. "I have. It's what encourages me. If I didn't play, I think I'd be eaten up with worry. Music has gotten me through many dark days. Or I should say God has. But he's used music to do it."

Betsy nodded, setting her empty juice glass on the floor. "What was your wife's name, Diederik?"

Diederik paused, closing his eyes as if remembering a thousand moments gone by. "Her name was Alida. It means noble." Running his fingers over the piano, her neighbour seemed lost in the past. "And that's what she was."

Betsy hoped he was all right and wondered whether she should change the subject, but her curiosity made her wait.

"I learned to play piano when I was a boy. And I loved it." Pausing, he took the hymnal and began to page through. "But then I got swept up in work and making money... you know..."

A tiny cuckoo clock sang the hour, but Betsy didn't move an inch.

"My father gave me and Alida this instrument when my mother died. He had no use for it… and to be honest, we thought we hadn't either. I shudder remembering how I almost didn't take it. We were too busy. Me especially. I thought I didn't need it. I thought I didn't need God. But then the car crash…"

Betsy reached out and touched the man's leathery hand.

"Alida and our son… they both died. All of a sudden, dollars and cents meant nothing. I grew very depressed and could hardly hold down a job. I just stayed in my house for weeks, feeling adrift. And as I sat in my living room, lonely and lost… I started playing. I hardly know how it happened. I started spending hours trying to get the chords right. The hymns… the truths… God imprinted each phrase on my mind and slowly rebuilt my heart. The truth of his Word shaped me into a whole new person. The lies had no power and his Word healed me."

Nodding, Betsy understood. God had worked similarly in her. Through Diederik's music and her learning to play, he'd reminded her of his presence and given her strength.

But there were moments when she still struggled to believe. She could sing a song, but sometimes the words fell flat.

"I don't always feel God, Diederik. I don't always believe the words in this book."

She expected shock, but instead Diederik nodded knowingly. Understanding shone in his kind eyes.

"Me too," he said. "When my wife died, I didn't feel or believe anything except my own hurt."

Betsy waited.

"But I chose to keep playing." He paused again. "The thing about truth… is it's true no matter what. We must stand firm in it, no matter what we feel or experience."

"That's hard."

Diederik's eyes brimmed with compassion. "Brutal sometimes. But when we trust the Lord and keep our mind on him despite our feelings… we have peace."

Betsy had a lot of feelings she didn't want, and she also wished she had feelings she didn't have. She felt anxious and afraid and longed to feel God more. But if Diederik was right, she could choose to believe the truth. Hadn't it sustained her thus far?

She thought of her husband, children, Sem… their secrets. It all felt like too much, but perhaps she could once again lean on the Lord and trust his truth above every feeling in her heart.

Tears welled in her eyes, but they weren't tears of sadness. They were tears of relief, tears of peace. She didn't have to carry the weight of the world or the weight of their situation.

Always a gentleman, Diederik reached into his pocket and retrieved his handkerchief. He handed it to her.

Standing, he took their glasses and returned with mugs of coffee.

Twenty minutes later, she headed for home. Hank and the children were playing outside and Betsy quickly got to work on supper. As she scrubbed and chopped her carrots, she smiled to herself. Yes, she was still afraid, but peace had settled over her. She felt light, for she didn't carry her heavy burdens anymore. She'd given them up to the Lord.

When Hank appeared to wash up for supper, he studied her for a moment. "You seem happy," he mused.

Betsy nodded. "I'm at peace."

Joy shone in her husband's eyes.

They called the children to supper and then Hank signalled Sem. Two coughs meant food. One cough meant he could use the restroom. Three meant danger.

"May it never be, Lord," Betsy prayed, and once again fear knocked on her door. Resisting, she cast it on the Lord, a habit she'd have to keep building.

♪♫♪

Betsy's headaches were growing more frequent. She felt tired and weak, and both she and Hank were worried. While she'd resisted going to the doctor for a long time, she could do so no longer.

"No more excuses," Hank had told her. "We're going to the clinic."

After dropping the children off at Janet's, they made their way downtown. Betsy hated this. The doctor's office always reminded her of her mother's illness, and it seemed there were reminders of war everywhere she looked. A motorcycle courier zoomed past and army vehicles dotted the streets.

Pulling up to the clinic, Betsy sighed. She remembered going there often, sitting in the waiting room while her mother underwent tests and spoke with a physician in hushed tones. Now it was Betsy's turn to see the doctor, and she naturally feared the worst.

Her mother had always reminded her that cancer ran in the family. She hadn't meant to scare her daughter. She had just wanted her to be wise and stay healthy.

But Betsy remembered the signs, and she was seeing them play out in her own body.

Hank helped her out of the vehicle and they walked inside. The receptionist ushered them into a waiting room, and a few minutes later the doctor entered and asked them some questions. He acted as if nothing was wrong with the world, as if they were just at a social gathering, not dealing with possible disease.

Betsy hung on to Hank's hand as if her life depended on it.

"I'd like you to go for some screening," the doctor finally said, still smiling.

"Do you think it's… cancer?" Betsy could barely say the dirty word. The smell of anaesthetic and bleach was ushering in another headache.

The doctor shook his head. "I don't know, Mrs. Vischer. From what you've told me… your symptoms, the lump on your breast, your mother's illness, and from what I can ascertain from this exam… I'd say it's very possible. But the tests will give us more information."

It wasn't what Betsy wanted to hear. She and Hank left the examination room and headed out to their waiting vehicle. Climbing in, Hank didn't speak. He started the engine and waited.

Clasping his hand, Betsy didn't want to meet his gaze, afraid of what she'd find there. Hadn't they been through enough?

"Lord, help," Hank whispered.

Betsy underwent many tests, and in a few weeks the results were in. It was cancer.

Chapter Nineteen

April 1943

"How're you feeling?" Hank joined his wife in their bedroom one night. They'd converted a closet into a room for Elizabeth, which meant they had their bedroom back to themselves.

Lying back against their wooden headboard, the one he'd made himself, Hank studied her. Betsy lay beside him, not knowing what to say. She was to have surgery two weeks from today and felt nervous. A spark of hope burned inside that maybe this would cure her. They'd remove her right breast in the hope of removing all cancer from her body.

But there were undeniable risks. What if something happened during the procedure? What if the disease had spread too far? What if Hank no longer found her attractive?

She clenched her eyes shut.

Hank lay beside her and put his arm around her shoulders. "I was reminiscing today."

"About what?" she asked, finally looking up.

"Our first date. Remember it? We went to the cinema, and then I walked you home."

Betsy laughed despite her weariness. "I was so nervous."

Hank laughed too. "I could tell. You wore a dress the colour of sunflowers."

Betsy grinned. "Everything was so good back then... so simple."

Hank ran his hand along the side of her face, even as the crickets sang outside their window.

"It still is," he whispered, kissing her head. His stubbly chin and calloused hands were a comfort. He touched her cheek. "Do you have strength to dance, my angel?"

Nodding, she took his hand.

♪♫♪

"Are you going to die, Mum?" John came to her one day as she sat folding laundry on the sofa. His two little siblings were blissfully playing in their sandbox, but worry now furrowed their older brother's brow.

"No, honey." She put down a shirt and took his hand. "The doctor just needs to fix Mummy up a little."

Her words fell flat. The truth was that she *didn't* know the outcome. She *didn't* know how long she had. She *didn't* know whether the surgery would go well at all.

But she understood her son's question and his need for reassurance. Lots of women had undergone this surgery. Her mother had as well and lived to see several years thereafter. From where she sat, she drew the boy close and John wrapped his long arms around her neck.

She and Hank had tried to explain things to the children. While they'd known their mother was sick, they didn't know the extent of it. At supper the night before, Hank had told them about her surgery and that they must pray and be very brave.

"I don't want anything to happen to you." John's lip was trembling.

She had recently cut his hair and she marvelled how much older it made him look.

Brushing away his tears, Betsy smiled sadly. "We mustn't be afraid, John," she whispered. "God is with us."

"Where is he?" her little son wanted to know. "I don't see him."

"We can't see him, but he's here." She pointed to her heart. "I've asked him to come live in me forever."

John titled his head thoughtfully. "Can he live in me forever too?"

Betsy nodded. "He sure can. You just have to ask him."

"I want to ask him," John confessed.

Beaming, Betsy took the little boy's hand.

May 1943

The day of the surgery arrived. Betsy awoke to sunlight streaming through the windowpane. Blinking, she rolled over, expecting to find Hank, but he wasn't there. What time was it? They had to be at the hospital by nine. Had she overslept?

Hearing the children's voices in the kitchen and then her husband's, she sat up, feeling the familiar discomfort. Her body ached and her head throbbed. The lump on her breast had gotten bigger, and her fear had grown with it.

The surgery wouldn't be simple, and the outcome wasn't sure. There could be complications, and the recovery would be long and hard even if everything went smoothly.

She glanced at her reflection across the room and realized she would look different. Her chest tightened. Would Hank look at her differently? He had always been so faithful, affectionate, and passionate. Would that change?

Forcing herself to stand, she moved across the warm wooden floor. It was a beautiful spring morning. Birds chirped outside her window, as if it were an ordinary day.

If it were only that.

Slipping from her nightgown, she stepped into her newest frock, something she'd sewn herself last fall. The colours reminded her of summers gone by. The baby blue fabric was embroidered with red roses and white carnations. She'd chosen soft ruby buttons down the front and the shoulders were boxy yet playful.

Taking a brush to her hair, she again looked in the mirror. Clothes would fit differently in a few hours. She'd have fewer curves, less shape… more ugliness. She tried to pin her hair up, but nothing seemed to look good.

Surrendering to a plain knot at the nape of her neck, she left the room and entered the kitchen. Her little daughter sat in the highchair, porridge spoon in hand and oatmeal all over her face. Upon seeing Betsy, she squealed and flung her next bite to the floor.

Betsy smiled too, figuring she'd clean the mess all at once after her daughter was fed. John and Henry were happily playing in the living room, their half-eaten breakfasts abandoned on the table.

Hank stood at the sink washing the oatmeal pot. "Rest well?"

He kissed her, a serious expression on his face.

She shrugged. Sleep had become fitful these past months, and last night had been the worst yet.

Her husband pointed to two bowls of oatmeal on the counter. "Try to eat something," he urged, glancing at the clock and avoiding her gaze again.

Sem appeared a moment later. Though he was often cold, his eyes were warmer today. "I hope all goes well."

"Thank you." Betsy played with her breakfast.

"We should be leaving soon," Hank told her, gathering their bags.

He again didn't make eye contact and Betsy's stomach churned. Was she already losing him? He knew what was coming. Nothing would ever be the same.

Janet's car pulled up outside. She'd be watching the children.

Betsy rose, grabbed a few last things, and then turned to her children as Janet slipped in through the door.

Before Betsy could leave any final instructions to her sister, John was by her side. "Don't leave, Mommy!" His big blue eyes pleaded with her.

Taking a deep breath, Betsy prayed for strength. She had known this moment would come and that it would be hard. Instead of replying quickly, she knelt beside him. Henry and Elizabeth came close as well. Drinking in the sight of them, she asked the Lord for wisdom.

"Mommy has to go and get better," she explained. "Remember what Daddy told you a few days ago?"

"You don't *seem* sick!" Henry crossed his arms.

He didn't know the half of it, though she was thankful she could keep a lot hidden.

"I *am* sick, Henry." She wouldn't lie to them. "But we must pray I get better soon." She turned to John. "Remember who will always be with you?"

John nodded, even as the usual tears rolled down his cheeks. "God."

Betsy nodded. "He will be with me, and he will be with you."

"How can he be in two places at once?" Henry wanted to know.

"It's a miracle, isn't it?" Betsy smiled. She prayed for more miracles every day.

Standing, she turned to Janet.

"Don't worry about a thing," her sister said with a smile. Then her voice dropped. "Just get better."

"Will do," Betsy whispered. "There's lunch in the refrigerator that just needs to be heated up." She pointed to a stack of books on the table. "And the boys have a little homework."

Janet nodded, and Hank motioned that they needed to go. Kissing her children, Betsy headed to the vehicle.

The surgery was to be performed at the Utrecht hospital, so they had a bit of a drive ahead. Hank turned out of town onto the main road and they drove in silence for some time.

Looking out the window, Betsy's chin trembled. It wasn't that she was afraid of the surgery itself. Several women she knew had undergone it, and the doctor was good. No, she was afraid for what came after. If the surgery didn't go well or the cancer had spread further than they thought, how would her children bear losing their mother? How would Hank manage on his own?

She was also afraid for her marriage. If the operation were successful, would Hank even be attracted to her anymore? If they had forty or fifty more years together, as she prayed they did, would he look at her the same way? The question plagued her and she didn't have an answer.

As they approached the outskirts of the city, they came in sight of a German checkpoint. "What's this?" her husband queried.

Betsy took his free hand and held it tight.

Rolling down the window, they watched as a German soldier and Dutch policeman approached.

"Good morning," the Dutchman nodded.

"Hello," Hank answered coldly. "What's going on?"

"We're just doing a routine check," the man explained, motioning to his clipboard and the several military vehicles nearby.

The soldier said something in German and began circling the vehicle for inspection.

The policeman turned to Hank. "Where're you headed this fine day? What brings you to Utrecht?"

"The hospital. My wife is having an operation." Hank almost choked on the word.

The man looked at Betsy, a flicker of compassion in his eyes. Clearing his throat, he turned to his clipboard. "I'll need some ID from both of you."

They produced what was requested and within minutes were on their way again.

It took some time for Betsy to catch her breath, but her pulse quickened again as they pulled into the hospital parking lot.

Hank killed the engine and turned to her. "Are you all right?"

"I'm afraid," she whispered. "But it's not what you think."

He waited.

Looking him straight in the eye, she asked the question that burned in her mind. "Will you love me the same after it's all over?"

She knew she sounded childish, but she couldn't help herself. Her fears felt colossal.

Hank's lined brow wrinkled and he took her small hand in his calloused one. "What kind of question is that?"

"An honest one."

"I've loved you since the day I met you," he murmured.

She smiled. "At the church? When you horrified Janet with your heathen ways?"

He chuckled. "Did I horrify you?"

"Not in the slightest. Then you sneezed so loudly the whole congregation heard."

"My father heard."

Betsy frowned as the sad memories came back.

"He took me around back and gave me a good whipping," he murmured.

Her little heart had broken for the boy.

Hank looked at her, really looked. He had a way of staring into her soul, seeing all the fear and brokenness and loving her still. She'd always wondered how he did so, how he loved her and believed the best about her.

As if knowing her thoughts, he spoke again. "My father never really loved me. I think it was because he never experienced real love himself. He was always brittle, eager to punish and never forgive. I didn't know any different... until I met you. You were gracious, and that made me want to be gracious."

Betsy smiled, but fear still gripped her. "I won't look the same, Hank," she whispered, hating to bring it up again but still plagued by her own anxieties.

Hank nodded, understanding what she meant. He wrapped his arms around her and pulled her close. "Will you still have the same nose?"

Taken aback, Betsy laughed. "Of course!"

Running his finger down her nose, he reached her lips. "Will these change?"

She shook her head.

He moved his hand to her heart. "And I have it on good authority you'll still have the kindest, gentlest heart in the world."

Leaning her head on his shoulder, she exhaled. She didn't deserve him.

Chapter Twenty

The doctor said the surgery was successful. "It looked like we were able to catch things before they went too far," he told them. "But we'll keep an eye on it. We may not be in the clear yet."

Betsy was thankful for what seemed like a positive outcome and prayed it'd stay that way.

They remained in Utrecht for almost a week before heading home, and she remained bedridden for a while after that. Hank, Janet, and the children waited on her attentively.

But while the situation at home felt hopeful, the war was getting worse. The Germans had been slowly confiscating their freedoms and getting more stringent. The authorities were now taking away everyone's radios.

"They can't do this," Betsy breathed, sitting in her armchair one day while eyeing her beloved radio from across the room. It was the one Hank had given her at the dance all those years ago. It was the tiniest radio she'd ever seen and it had made her heart melt. He'd fixed it up and they'd listened to it for hours at a time.

Henry stomped his foot. "It's not fair!"

"Not fair!" Elizabeth echoed.

"How will we listen to our shows now?" John beseeched.

The three children had been working on a puzzle, but now they stood facing her, their task long forgotten.

Betsy bit her lip. They hadn't had many shows to listen to for quite some time, at least nothing that wasn't German propaganda. Hank, on the other hand, had still found ways to listen to the news. He'd gather information and print it in pamphlets to distribute to those who needed it. The truth was that Betsy didn't know half of what her husband did, and it was for her safety that he didn't disclose much.

Slowly pulling herself to her feet, Betsy reached for the radio on the shelf. Perhaps it was silly to feel so attached to a machine, yet this contraption represented so much more than evening music programs. It represented Hank's love and their freedom. So many family memories revolved around it.

Never wanting to disobey and always wanting to comply and keep the peace, Betsy hesitated. She ran her finger along the antenna, contemplating her next move.

"I hate the Germans," Henry said.

"Watch your words, my son" Betsy instinctively reprimanded him, yet deep inside she did too. Hadn't she offered a cold shoulder to Ada and her German boyfriend? Hadn't she wished horrible things on so many?

"But it's not fair, Mum!"

Betsy nodded. "I know."

She knew her son's grief, for she carried the load herself. She wanted to raise her children to respect others, and she wanted to demonstrate Christ's love. But what would Christ do? Would he bend the knee to these demands? When did justice need to be fought for? When did someone need to stand up?

Hank seemed to have it all figured out, but Betsy had a few more questions.

Yet she knew what to do now. She took the radio and put it in the drawer. It would stay there.

June 1943

"Lightly, Henry. Pour lightly."

Sticking out his tongue in a sign of intense focus, her son tipped the huge can over the carrot plants, showering them with water.

It had been a month since the operation and Betsy was starting to feel more like herself. She was glad to be able to get outside, but she was thankful for her children's help with the chores. Henry particularly liked to help water the plants, although she had to keep an eye on him to make sure he didn't drown them.

"You're getting so big, Henry," a familiar voice spoke behind her. *Eliana.*

Turning quickly, Betsy saw the young woman approach. Henry dropped his watering can and ran to her side. Eliana was quick to retrieve it before the water completely sopped the stems.

Eyes filling with tears, Betsy stared at the girl. She hadn't seen her in ages, hadn't even heard from her. Pulling herself to her feet, she went towards her.

"It's been so long," Betsy breathed.

Eliana turned to her, something unknown in her eyes. Kind, faithful, hard-working Eliana also carried a burden. Betsy didn't know what it was.

"I'm sorry I just disappeared. Life has been... scary."

Betsy nodded, understanding a little. The Jews were being targeted and even sent away to ghettos in Amsterdam.

"Shall we go inside?" Betsy asked.

Eliana quickly nodded. "I was hoping you'd say that."

The three of them headed into the kitchen, and John and Elizabeth gave an equally boisterous welcome as their brother. Betsy set the kettle to boil and pulled a cookie out of the jar.

"I want one!" Henry squealed.

"Me too!" Elizabeth chimed in.

Usually Betsy would say no, but today felt different and she prayed for wisdom. Taking three more cookies out of the jar, she closed the lid. She placed the treats in a clean dishcloth and handed them to her eldest.

"You children go play outside. Eliana and I will come find you in a bit."

Happy for the cookies but reluctant to go, the three obeyed.

Betsy set the table and made some tea. When she finally sat down, she couldn't wait a moment longer.

She took the girl's hand. "What's going on, Eliana?"

"I need... help," her friend whispered. She dropped her gaze. "I need...a place to stay."

A knot formed in Betsy's stomach.

The girl eyed her tea and continued. "I tried to go stay with my aunt, but it's too dangerous to travel."

Betsy understood. Eliana didn't just want to stay with them—she wanted to hide in their house, to find refuge within their walls.

"My father was taken." The girl's voice trembled.

Betsy put a hand on the girl's shoulder. "I'm so sorry, friend."

Eliana couldn't speak for a moment. Hadn't the girl been through enough?

"My mother went to stay with a friend, but they only have room for one. It's not safe for me at home. It doesn't feel safe anywhere..." She looked up at Betsy. "Except here."

For who knows how long? Betsy wanted to say. Her heart yearned to care for the girl, and she was happy her friend felt safe here...

But there was a risk. If Eliana stayed with them, they would again be putting their lives in danger. Hers would be another mouth to feed, another person to hide, another reason to worry.

For a moment, Betsy wanted to say no. She wanted to take her children and her husband and run away from all of this.

Just as quickly as that thought came, she remembered something: on the day that Eliana had told her of Samuel's death, she'd prayed that God would show her what to do. She hadn't had much of an answer then... but she'd waited. Her burden hadn't lifted when Sem had come to live with them. Now her mission was clear. She'd have to talk to Hank, but she already knew what his answer would be.

Of course Eliana could stay with them.

The door opened with a bang and Henry practically flew inside. "Eliana, come see my train!" he begged.

Eliana turned to the boy and tried to fix his cowlick. "I'd love to see it."

Standing, the girl followed Henry to the door, but before going out she turned and looked back at Betsy. Though apprehensive, Betsy nodded. Even though she was uneasy, a strange peace settled over her.

The girl exhaled.

When Eliana and Henry were gone, Betsy lingered alone at the table. They were in over their heads, of that she was certain. To anyone watching, their lives were riddled with pain, risk, fear, and difficulty, yet Betsy had peace. She had joy, in fact. It wasn't that she was unafraid, but she'd grown to believe something greater than her anxiety: God was kind and in control, and they would be okay.

August 1943

As food ran low, prices skyrocketed. Everyone seemed to be struggling and Betsy thanked the Lord that they could grow their own vegetables and herbs.

But while she enjoyed the fresh greens, sometimes the children complained about their simple meals.

"Why must we just eat vegetables?" Henry whined one day at supper. He poked at his helping of greens and even let a piece of cucumber drop to the floor.

"That's enough, Henry," Betsy reprimanded.

"And we don't just eat vegetables," Hank added, pointing to the boiled beans beside him. "These will make you big and strong, my boy."

Henry looked at his father in disbelief.

"I eat beans every day," Hank continued, taking a mouthful. "They're quite delicious."

Tilting his head, her son contemplated doing the same.

Betsy smiled to herself. Her husband didn't like beans at all, and for the first several years of their marriage she'd avoided cooking with them. But since they were the cheapest protein she could find and they kept a long while without spoiling, they now ate them quite often. Her husband never complained, and it made Betsy love him even more.

Finally, Henry took a spoonful. If his father liked beans, they must be delicious.

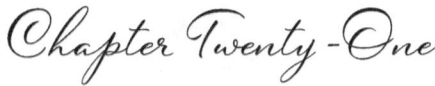

Chapter Twenty-One

September 1943

Betsy read to Elizabeth at the table, a stack of books by their side. The boys had gone off to school and Hank was out on business, whether fixing radios or doing something illegal, she did not know.

"They might question you, Betsy," he had told her. "The less you know, the safer you'll be."

Betsy understood, but she also worried. Hank's life was in danger.

The Nazis were trying to control the information that went out and Hank was actively seeking to stop their efforts. If people were unaware, they were defenceless. Hank had always wanted people to stay informed. He was passionate about giving people the chance to think for themselves.

In recent years, he'd also become passionate about thwarting Nazi communication. Though he never said so, Betsy believed that Hank had been commissioned to somehow sabotage Nazi radio lines. She prayed for his safety.

Betsy's heart dropped at the sound of a loud knock on the door. Her daughter bolted for the window and peered out. She loved company.

"Friends! Friends!" Elizabeth squealed.

For all Betsy knew, it *was* a friend.

But something inside told her otherwise. In fact, something inside her went cold. She dropped her gaze to the floor. Beneath her shoes, beneath the rug, were hidden two people she'd grown to care for. They'd come up briefly for breakfast and they'd just returned to their dark home.

Without hesitating, Betsy coughed three times. It was their signal—danger.

The knock came again and she heard muffled voices. Rising, she went to her daughter and picked her up. Her feet felt as heavy as bricks and the door handle cold as ice.

Please, Lord, protect us.

Opening the door, she came face to face with two men, one in uniform and the other wearing a dark coat. With brimmed hats, tall boots, and files in hand, there was no mistaking why they were here.

"Good morning, Betsy," the man on the right addressed her.

Surprised he knew her name, Betsy stared closer. She recognized him. It was none other than her old schoolmate.

"Bert?" Her greeting came out more like a question.

She glanced at his companion. He was taller, more grim and very German.

Sensing her mother's unease, Elizabeth tightened her grip around her neck.

"Sorry to bother you, Betsy," Bert said with a nod. "This will only take a minute."

Although she'd heard that many Dutch people had joined the German forces—Hannie's husband being one of them—Betsy hadn't seen Bert in years. He looked weathered and smaller than normal in his heavy uniform.

Betsy tried to sound calm. "What can I do for you?"

"We just want to ask you a few questions," Bert smiled, his teeth still crooked and yellow.

Opening the door wider, she let them in.

They entered solemnly and the German man said something to Bert.

"He says that you have a nice home." Bert eyed the bedroom and back door. "Hank around?"

Betsy marvelled that he even asked. Bert had never liked her husband, and she had always thought him jealous.

She subconsciously pulled her daughter closer to her chest. "No."

"Who are you?" little Elizabeth asked, finally getting up the courage to speak.

Bert grinned and casually wiped his dirty boots. "This must be your daughter. She looks like you."

Betsy nodded. It took all her willpower not to look over her shoulder, to the table and rug that hid their secret. But Bert did.

"What a lovely table." He moved towards it and said something to his companion in German. Then he looked back at Betsy. "Hank made it? He's always been good at that sort of thing."

The man in the trench coat stomped to the kitchen and peered out the back window.

Wondering if her voice would hold out and knowing her legs wouldn't, Betsy sat.

"Yes…" Her voice quavered. "It was a wedding gift."

"What a beauty," Bert mused, and Betsy felt her cheeks burn. For some reason, she felt he wasn't talking about the table.

He ran his hand along the smooth surface.

The man in the trench coat turned and spoke to Bert again, pointing to the file in his hand. Bert took it and looked up.

"We have a few people we're looking for, Betsy. Would you mind if I ran a few names by you?"

"What type of people?" Her voice felt hoarse.

"Troublemakers… I'm sure you don't know them." He chuckled. "Just routine, you know."

He then rattled off a few names… Abraham Cohen, Levi Oberman, and the last one: Sarah Sandler.

Betsy bit her lip. That was Eliana's mother.

"I've never met any of those people," she replied, for truthfully she had not.

For a split second, he eyed her doubtfully. Then he smiled and closed his file. "Thank you for your cooperation, Betsy. I was sure we wouldn't find anything here. You're too wise a woman to go against the law. Those who rebel put their whole families at risk."

Swallowing, she nodded.

"Do you have any tea?" he asked. "We've got several more errands before lunch."

Surprised and overwhelmed, Betsy stood. She set the kettle to boil, trying to stop her hands from trembling. Retrieving two teacups, she had to work one-handed as Elizabeth clung to her.

Swallowing her guilt, she left the full cookie jar untouched.

They drank their tea at a turtle's pace. The men downed two cups each.

Betsy held Elizabeth and prayed for the girl's discretion. Thankfully, her daughter was too shy to speak further.

When the men were gone, Elizabeth turned to her. "Mama?"

"Hush now," Betsy told her. Who knew how long the men would stick around outside? Who knew what they'd hear?

Giving up on her daughter's breakfast, Betsy brought the dish to the sink and set about changing Elizabeth out of her nightgown. The girl's fine hair was a shimmering gold. She ran a little comb through it and did her best to pin it into place.

Afterward she watched her toddle into the living room to play, hairpins flying everywhere.

Realizing she'd been holding her breath, Betsy finally exhaled. Rather than following her daughter, she fell to her knees. She closed her eyes and felt tears slip through.

"Thank you," she whispered.

God had protected them. He had answered her prayer.

But what Bert had said lingered in her memory. *"You're too wise a woman to go against the law."* Hearing her daughter's babble, she recalled the rest: *"Those who rebel put their whole families at risk."*

She wrapped her arms around herself and tried to ward off her fears. *We'll be all right,* she tried to tell herself, but perhaps they wouldn't.

As if water were rising within her, she started to drown in her anxiety and could hardly come up for air.

She couldn't breathe, couldn't think, couldn't see.

Help!

Betsy hadn't suffered a panic attack in a long time, but this one felt bad. Crumpling into a ball, she held her knees close to her chest and shut her eyes tight.

Help!

She felt her heartbeat throbbing in her head. Heat overwhelmed her body and she tried to rid herself of her sweater. Everything was too much. She couldn't go on.

It finally escaped her lips. "Help!"

"Mama?" Elizabeth's voice sounded far, far away.

Betsy wanted Hank. No, she wanted to die.

Jesus!

It was all she could do to open her eyes.

"Mama!" Elizabeth called for her, her chubby arms wrapping around her own.

Gulping, gasping, Betsy tried to hoist herself up.

"Jesus, help me," she breathed.

Taking her daughter's hand, they went to the back door and opened it. Suddenly, the sound of piano music reached her ears. Diederik was at it again.

She turned and looked across the fence. His window was open, though the air was far too warm for his liking.

Taking a deep breath, she understood the truth. He'd seen the men. He'd known her fears, opened his window, and began to play.

The Lord had heard her prayer.

Chapter Twenty-Two

Was the cancer really all gone? Betsy felt deep down that something still wasn't right. Had they really removed everything? If so, why did she still feel so drained?

Hank had insisted that they book another appointment and she'd finally acquiesced. They were to see the doctor in a week. She would somehow get through till then, resting as much as she could while leaving more strenuous tasks to others.

She absentmindedly mentioned harvesting the garden to her older sister. The cucumbers looked juicy and ripe. The beans were just waiting to be picked and the courgettes were bigger than ever.

"I'll harvest it," Janet informed her.

"I can't ask you to do that," Betsy replied.

"You didn't ask. I'm telling you."

Betsy could never argue with her older sister.

Janet now stood in her bedroom door, gloves on, smiling. "I'm ready to get at it," she said with a grin. It had been a long time since Betsy had seen her sister smile.

Elizabeth played contentedly with her toys; the boys were at school, and, generosity never ceasing, Janet had brought over bread dough which now baked in the oven. The smell wafted through the house, making Betsy's mouth water.

Betsy patted the blue and white quilt on her bed. "Come join me for a moment."

"I've no time to chat, Betsy. There're carrots to be unearthed."

The two laughed. "I'm not asking. I'm telling you," Betsy retorted, surprised by her own cheekiness.

Chuckling, Janet gave in and moved towards her. She sat down on the bed, her features softening. "How've you been feeling?"

"I think there's more cancer."

Janet dropped her head and played with the tattered edges of the blanket. "This needs mending. I'll bring my good needles tomorrow."

She took her sister's rough hand. "I'm scared, Janet. What about my children? You know how hard it was growing up with Mother sick. She missed out on so much... and then we lost her."

"Hush, Betsy." Her sister pulled her hand away. "You're not dead."

Her words were harsh. Some people were intimidated by Janet's manner, but Betsy knew her sister loved her. Janet's kindness was palpable. It just came in thunderbolts.

"I might die sooner than I'd like," she whispered. Although she was excited to meet the Lord, she feared leaving people behind. "What if I can't be there for my children? What if they don't remember me?"

Her older sister took her hand again. "No use worrying."

"I can't help it."

"Just stop it."

Betsy sighed. Her sister had a knack for stuffing down emotions, whether it was wise or not. Betsy, on the other hand, often felt led by her feelings. While she had learned to cast her anxieties on the Lord, doing so sometimes felt impossible.

Seeing her restlessness, Janet lay down beside her, like they used to do as girls.

"What do you remember most about Mother?" her older sister asked.

Betsy was surprised by the question but not stumped by it. Her answer came quickly: "Her love. How God's kindness shone through her."

Janet nodded. "I think that's how your children will remember you. You have a knack for love, Betsy—something I have to labour for."

Betsy shook her head. "Oh Janet—"

"Let me finish. Your children may not remember everything. Certain details may fade with time. But you love them, and you love God." She was quiet for a moment. "They'll remember God."

Drawing a deep breath, Betsy knew it was true, and it was enough. She longed to be with her children, to witness their futures unfold. She wanted to see John go to university and Henry bring a girl home and Elizabeth walk down the aisle on her father's arm.

She drew in a shaky breath.

Her sister took her hand and squeezed it. "But you're not gone yet," she finally said.

The two lay together a moment more before Janet headed out to the garden. As her sister began harvesting, Betsy breathed a prayer of gratitude. Her sister still didn't know about Sem or Eliana. Perhaps she could tell her one day. But what her sister did know was how to care well. Betsy prayed that the Lord would bless her.

Her sister worked tirelessly all morning. Around eleven, Betsy started on lunch. Though she felt weak, she was able to make some sandwiches, but how was she to get the food to Sem and Eliana? Janet could come in at any minute and discover their secret.

Janet came in and slipped off her work gloves. She washed her hands and dried them on an old tea towel.

"This is what you dry dishes with?" she asked Betsy in disbelief.

Betsy sighed, filling her water jug. "It does the job."

"I doubt that," her sister muttered.

Betsy knew there'd be a new set of dish towels on her doorstep soon, and it would be no use to protest.

Hank appeared from the shop, eyeing Betsy cautiously. She smiled, letting him know that their secret was still safe.

The children were called and Hank said the blessing. Tomato sandwiches without butter weren't anyone's favourite, but thankfully no one made a fuss.

They had just about cleared their plates when the clock struck twelve.

"Have you heard from Eliana lately?" Janet asked.

Betsy felt the blood drain from her face.

"Elee-ana!" Elizabeth echoed.

Betsy turned quickly to her husband, wondering how to respond. "Not in some time," she replied, the words as sour as lemons on her tongue.

Hank rose and cleared the plates. The children stared at her, more than a little confused. Janet eyed her suspiciously. Did her sister not believe it? If anyone could read her, it was Janet.

Standing to her feet, Betsy wiped her children's mouths.

"I'm heading off on some errands," her husband said.

He finished the dishes, then kissed her. A knowing look passed between them and then he was off.

"And I'll get back to it," Janet murmured, once again putting on her gloves and returning to the garden.

Betsy retrieved two clean plates and assembled more sandwiches.

Protect us, Father.

Quickly motioning to her eldest son, they noiselessly moved the table and rolled back the rug. Betsy coughed twice. The trapdoor opened and Eliana and Sem appeared.

"Thank you," Eliana whispered.

"We'll be quiet until she leaves," Sem murmured.

But all of a sudden, the back door opened.

Janet stared at her. She wasn't normally speechless, but she was now.

"You can't tell a soul, Janet," Betsy whispered, unable to bear the thought that she might.

Sem glared at her sister. Though Eliana was a little more trusting, even she now held her breath.

Janet shifted from one foot to the other, contemplating the situation. She looked at the children, then at Sem and Eliana, and then finally back at Betsy.

"You're putting your family in danger," Janet said. "You know that, right?"

Betsy swallowed, nodding.

"How long have they been staying with you?"

"Sem has been here almost two years," Betsy replied. "Eliana came to us last fall."

Janet's eyes widened.

"Are you going to tell the authorities?" Sem asked coldly. "How do we know we can trust you?"

Janet was neither intimidated nor moved by the man's words. She stood still, forever resolute but unusually thoughtful.

Finally, she turned to Sem. "You have my word. I won't tell."

"How am I to believe that?" Sem retorted.

"You can believe her," Betsy assured him. If Janet was anything, she was trustworthy.

Sem and Eliana sat down to eat while Janet washed up at the sink.

"Have you been feeding them enough?" her sister whispered.

Betsy shrugged as she gave her plants on the windowsill a drink. "As much as we can. You know the shortages."

"That I do." Her sister dried her hands on the same tattered towel. "There's not a good piece of meat in a hundred miles."

Janet peered for a while at the two at the table.

"I have some extras." Janet had lowered her voice to a whisper. "Some tomatoes and apples in my cellar. I'll bring them by tomorrow."

Betsy drew in a deep breath. There her sister went again, taking care of them all. "I can't ask you to do that."

Janet smiled. "You didn't ask. I'm telling you."

Chapter Twenty-Three

October 1943

The day of the appointment arrived. Hank took her to the clinic. More tests were run and the results came back positive. There was more cancer, and it was spreading like wildfire. It seemed there wasn't much more they could do.

♫♪

Store shelves were practically empty, and the cupboards in Betsy's kitchen were much the same. Thankfully they had a jar or two of beans and a few vegetables in the root cellar, but she knew they wouldn't last long. Hank had heard of a butcher smuggling food to those in need and set out to see what he could get his hands on, but three days had passed and he had yet to return.

Janet had come to stay with them for a while and Betsy was grateful for her help.

Sitting in her room one afternoon, Betsy tried in vain to read. It seemed she couldn't focus these days. Her mind was so full of worry that it had no room for make-believe. Hearing her bedroom door squeak open, she turned to see a pair of little eyes peering through.

Betsy smiled. "Is that a tiny mouse I see?"

The door opened farther and there was little Henry, though he wasn't so little anymore. He was a full six years old and proud of it.

"I'm sorry, Betsy." Janet stood behind him. "I told him you were sleeping."

"It's okay, Janet. They can come in."

Knowing the others couldn't be far behind, Betsy pulled herself to a sitting position.

In a moment, there were her three children—Henry in the lead, Elizabeth at his heels, and John hesitantly behind. Janet left them in private.

"Are you sure you don't need to rest, Mama?" her seven-year-old son worried. Forever the sensitive and compliant sort, John wanted to do things right.

"I need to see my babies," Betsy assured him.

The three climbed up beside her.

"I'm not a baby!" Henry retorted.

Three-year-old Elizabeth chimed in. "I'm not a baby!"

"No, no. None of you are babies anymore. You're all big and strong."

"I *am* strong!" Henry agreed, flexing his arm. "I beat Sven in arm-wrestling yesterday."

"I'm so proud of you." Betsy turned to John. "How did your arithmetic test go?"

John dropped his head. "I got a B."

She lifted his chin. "That's excellent!"

"It wasn't an A."

Betsy tilted her head. He was so like herself—that was, before she'd experienced God's love. Like her son, she'd often been disappointed in herself and nitpicked every flaw.

Give him peace.

"I'm so proud of you," she whispered.

"Can you tell us a story?" Elizabeth implored, snuggling in.

Running her fingers through the girl's blond whisps, Betsy nodded. "Of course I can."

Betsy wondered where to start and recalled her favourite Bible story, the one about Naaman being healed of his leprosy.

"Naaman had a terrible disease called leprosy, and he desperately wanted to be healed. He was sent to the prophet Elisha. He thought maybe Elisha would wave his hand over him and make everything better. But do you know what the prophet told him?"

"Go take a bath!" Henry declared, laughing.

Betsy tugged his shirt. "I think I've told you the same thing a time or two."

"Henry gets stinky." Elizabeth wrinkled her nose and they all giggled.

"Elisha told Naaman to do something small, and perhaps it seemed insignificant. He told him to wash in the Jordan River—"

"—seven times!" Henry squealed.

Betsy nodded. "But when he came out of the water…"

John gave her a beatific smile. "He was healed."

"That's right, my son. Naaman wanted to pay Elisha for his healing. But what did Elisha say?"

Elizabeth knew that one. "He said no!"

"God loved Naaman," Betsy explained. "His healing was a gift."

"I like gifts," Henry declared.

"I do too," Betsy agreed. "We've been given lots of gifts, haven't we?"

"We don't get very many presents on St. Nicolas Day," he retorted.

Betsy nodded, knowing all too well how difficult life had been lately. "Sometimes gifts don't have bows and ribbons. In fact, I think the best gifts aren't wrapped up in paper at all."

"What kind of gifts aren't wrapped up in paper?" Henry queried in disbelief.

Betsy paused thoughtfully. "You three are gifts, and so is your father. Then there's Aunt Janet, this house, our food…" Her voice trailed off as a lump formed in her throat. She swallowed hard. "And God's love. We don't have to work for God's love. He just gives it to us. It's the most wonderful gift of all."

John leaned against her arm and sighed. "I miss Daddy."

Betsy couldn't speak. While she knew it was unsafe for her husband to call home, she wished he would. Hearing his voice would ease her fears and quiet her imagination.

"When will Daddy be home?" Henry wanted to know.

"I pray soon." It was all she could manage.

The Lord's gifts were his to give and take, but the thought of losing her husband felt like more than she could bear.

The night was colder than usual. Her bed felt too big and her room too empty.

Where in the world was her husband? Why hadn't he come home by now? What if he had gotten caught and she never saw him again? She would have to raise their children alone. But then what if the illness took her? They would be orphaned.

Shivering, she slid further under the covers.

She turned towards the window and found it dark. The light of the moon had almost disappeared.

How could she go on without Hank Vischer? She couldn't bear to think about it, yet her thoughts kept spinning.

Why would you give him to me just to take him away? she prayed. *Why would you take their father? How would I ever go on without him?*

Hank was a rock. He loved her and ministered so much peace to her heart. He could make her laugh even when everything felt dark inside, and when he held her the world calmed down.

Burying her face to mute her sobs, she gave in. Sometimes crying helped, but other times she lost control. Hank had always known how to comfort her, but he was gone.

Unable to draw a full breath, she felt despair once again take over.

"Help," she managed in a whisper.

She needed to ground herself, to stand up, to move, but she felt paralyzed and her body was weak.

She said it a little louder this time. "Help."

Was she dying? It felt like it.

Suddenly, the door squeaked open.

"Little sister?"

Janet was there. She turned on a lamp, illuminating the room. Betsy knew she had to open her eyes, but it felt impossible to do anything but give in to sorrow.

"Look at me, little sister."

She felt Janet take her hand.

Blinking, Betsy obeyed.

"It's all too much, Janet," she whispered hoarsely. "I can't bear this… not knowing where he is… not knowing what's going to happen. What if… what if I die?" Her words came quicker and she struggled to take a full breath. "What if the children don't remember me? What if they lose us both? What if the authorities find out—"

"That's enough," Janet stopped her. "Look at me, little sister."

Betsy realized she'd closed her eyes again.

Janet pulled back the covers and helped her sit up. "Remember Mother's favourite song. Remember the truth…"

Betsy nodded and took a shaky breath. *Rock of Ages*. They had sung it at her funeral and often spoke of how it ministered to them.

"Would you sing it, Janet?" she asked.

Janet was hesitant, but only for a moment.

Rock of Ages, cleft for me,
Let me hide myself in Thee;
Let the water and the blood,
From Thy wounded side which flowed,
Be of sin the double cure,
Save from wrath and make me pure.[6]

Betsy breathed again, deeper this time. Hank was gone and God might take him away for good. But she knew the truth: she had Jesus.

Though her heart broke, she opened her hands. Another tear escaped her and she surrendered her husband.

Let me hide myself in Thee.

---

[6] Augustus Montague Toplady, "Rock of Ages," 1763.

Chapter Twenty-Four

Betsy felt as though her heart stopped. It was nearly ten o'clock the following night and everyone had gone to bed, yet she heard the front door squeak open.

Not knowing whether Janet was awake, she tried to pull herself from bed as quickly as she could. Her body moved slowly, but the galloping of her heart spurred her on.

She opened the bedroom door, bracing for whatever she would see.

"Hank," she breathed.

It was him.

He turned to her and she felt herself crumble. Taking her in his arms, Hank kissed her, and she revelled in the smell of him.

"My love, my love," she whispered as her body trembled next to his.

All the worry, fear, and sadness she'd held onto for so long could fully come out at last.

"I'm home," he replied.

Her legs couldn't hold her any longer and Hank swept her up and carried her back to bed. The bed creaked as he sat down beside her.

She took his hand. "You've been gone so long."

"I promised myself I wouldn't return without food, but it was so hard to come by." His calloused hand felt cold.

"Did you find anything?"

He nodded. "A little. I wanted to get more, but..."

"But?"

"It's not safe, Betsy. The authorities know who I am... what I've been doing these past years."

Betsy bit her lip. She didn't even know the extent of her husband's work, yet she knew enough... enough to know what this meant. Hank's life was in danger. They would be looking for him.

"What should we do?" she asked.

"I have to go underground."

"You mean hide?"

"No one must know I'm here, Betsy." His words brooked no argument, and she didn't try. "As far as anyone is concerned, I've gone away. Our friends, our family, no one must know I'm home."

"Will they come searching for you?"

"I don't know. I pray to God they won't. Who knows what would happen then?"

Betsy stared at her husband, but she barely recognized him. He'd grown so thin. While he was living his passion and seemed to be doing what he was always meant to do, he was also tired. The weight of it all was beginning to crush him.

"Are you okay, my love?"

Hank turned and looked her straight in the eye. Though he rarely cried, his blue eyes clouded. "I'm fighting the old lies, Betsy. Things people told me... what people labelled me as... useless, lazy, incapable... I feel like a failure. I can't even provide for my family, and now I have to run and hide."

Now Betsy took hold of his other hand. "Would you lie with me?"

He nodded and they lay down together. Wrapping her arms around him, like he'd done so many times, she leaned her head on his chest and listened to his heartbeat. His heart was beautiful yet broken. How she longed to mend it!

Give me the words, she prayed.

"When you were little, how did you see God?"

He knew where she was going. "Harsh, small, waiting to punish my every mistake."

"How do you see him now?" She ran her finger along his stubbly chin.

"He loves me."

"So whose voice have you been listening to?"

Hank sighed just as the wind outside joined in. "Not his."

She smiled. "It's not too late to change the channel."

May 1944

The town hall was bustling. A line of men and women had gathered at a large desk and Betsy waited her turn. Though her body begged her to sit, she willed herself to persevere.

When she reached the front of the queue, the clerk nodded and asked for her name.

"Henry and Elizabeth Vischer," Betsy told the man, producing a piece of ID.

A man in uniform found her name on his clipboard and produced a tiny card.

"Next!" he called, and she moved aside.

Eyeing the small print and tear-off tabs, she swallowed hard. Would this get them through? Would they have enough groceries to feed not just their family but Sem and Eliana too? Even with Janet's contributions, it was getting harder to make do.

She suddenly heard a familiar voice behind her: "Betsy?"

Looking up, she saw her brother-in-law Isaak. Dressed in a suit and tie with a Nazi political party pin on his lapel, he strode towards her.

"How are you all?" he asked.

"Good," she replied too quickly.

"How's Hank?"

Even though he smiled, Betsy felt strangely threatened. Was he simply asking after family or was he fishing for something more?

"He's been gone lots," she said truthfully.

There was a pause and Isaak stared at her for a moment. Something didn't look right in his eyes, but she couldn't put her finger on it.

Then, just as quickly as the feeling had come, it faded, and she saw nothing but kindness.

"Good to see you." He smiled and made his way back to his office.

Betsy knew she should've asked about Hannie and the children. She knew she had acted suspiciously. She hated keeping secrets from her family and believing they were keeping secrets from her.

Have mercy, she prayed as she made her way out.

November 1944

"I want butter on my toast!" Henry whined the next morning. He stubbornly sat at the table, though his siblings had been finished long ago. John was on his bed reading and Elizabeth played with her dolls in the living room. Having refused his toast and hashbrowns, Betsy hadn't allowed Henry to leave until he finished.

"We don't have butter," Betsy tried to explain. "No one does."

She hoped that would help ease the loss. Her son liked to compare his lot with his friends at school. He would tell them how Sven had had beef for dinner or Willem had had cheese, but no one had those things now. Meat had disappeared... then cheese... now butter. She wondered how many meals they could make with bread and potatoes. Though she was a fine cook and had learned to be creative, bread and potatoes could only be interesting for so long.

Her husband appeared and she poured his coffee. He'd started working in the basement to avoid discovery. Though he himself looked tired, he noticed Betsy's concern.

"What is it?" he asked, taking the cup from her hands and putting it to his lips.

Eyeing the open refrigerator, she whispered, "This won't be enough, Hank. It will barely get us through a few days, much less till we get our next rations."

Nodding, he set down his coffee cup and went for his coat.

"Where are you going?" she asked.

"I'll find more."

Racing after him, she grasped his arm. Was she going to lose him again? "What do you mean, Hank? No one has food, and it's not safe..."

He slipped on his coat and scarf. "There's a farming town just a few miles east. Word is they have bread and milk... maybe even some meat. Trucks can't reach them, but people can."

Betsy knew it would be illegal, taking more than their ration. Her husband could get arrested and her pulse quickened at the thought.

"No," she stammered, grabbing his arm. "It's too risky."

"Where are you going, Dad?" Henry called, jumping down from his chair. "I want to come!"

"You stay here, son. Finish your breakfast!"

"I want to come too!" Elizabeth dropped her dolls on the sofa.

Softening, Hank picked up both children.

Betsy studied her husband. "There're other ways, Hank. Janet's starting a soup kitchen. We can go there—"

Hank stopped her. "I can provide."

Betsy loved Hank's confidence, sacrificial heart, and sense of duty, but he was also proud—and she feared he'd pay for it.

As if on cue, her stomach growled. She *was* famished, and the children were too. It was even hard to sleep at night because of it. She wished they had more. They *needed* more.

She also longed to bring Diederik some food. She hadn't seen him in a while and knew he was unwell. In fact, there were many people who had much less than them. If only she could help!

Reading her thoughts, Hank set the children down and took her head in his hands. Kissing her, he smiled. "Have Janet bring you all to the soup kitchen, and then take some of our rations to Diederik."

She nodded. He too cared about the old man.

"I'll be back in a day or two."

Chapter Twenty-Five

December 1944

Betsy heard their boots. She saw the all-too-familiar car outside... and she knew.

Sem was in the living room reading and Eliana had been helping her with laundry. There was a lot of it these days. Henry and Elizabeth were out back and John was drying the lunch dishes for her.

At the sound of banging on the door, Betsy jumped. She turned to Sem and Eliana, but they were already gone, disappearing beneath the trapdoor and silently pulling it closed.

Betsy arranged the rug in place.

Eyes wide, John stared at her. "Mama?" her eight-year-old son beseeched her.

"Shh," she quieted him, motioning him to help her move the table back. "Go watch your siblings."

All three children knew their reality, but Betsy still feared what they might accidentally say. Perhaps if they stayed outside, they wouldn't be questioned.

When her son had gone, she opened the door. Two men met her on the other side, one older and one who looked to be in his mid-twenties.

The first man smiled. "Good morning, Mrs. Vischer."

Betsy wanted to crawl inside herself. He knew her name. She'd never get used to them all knowing her name.

"It's a little chilly out," he said. "May we come in?"

Heart racing, she moved aside. They stepped into the living room and looked around with ease. Hanging up their coats, they didn't bother to wipe their boots.

The older one strode to the table and sat down. The other went to the window overlooking the backyard.

"Are those your children?" the first man asked. "How old are they?"

Betsy told them.

The man at the table laughed. "Not quite old enough for the Hitler Youth."

"But he would make a good soldier," interjected the one at the window.

Betsy shuddered.

"Tall and strong?" the older man queried.

"And blond to boot." The other turned to Betsy. "Do you have something to eat?"

Betsy swallowed. They didn't have enough to share.

"Yes, yes," the other agreed. "Surely you could spare a bit of toast."

"And jam perhaps?" The first began opening cupboards.

It felt like more than she could bear. Anger rose up inside her and Betsy wanted to scream. What made them think they could just come in like this and ask for whatever they wished? She wasn't their slave.

"What I wouldn't give for a cup of coffee." The man at the table sighed, putting up his feet.

I can't do this, Lord.

Betsy moved towards the cupboard. Opening the oven, she laid two slices of bread inside and got them heating. Her hands shook as she measured out some coffee and got the kettle boiling.

"Do you keep the jam in the cellar?" the man at the table asked, his words cold and suspicious.

She froze. They *did* keep a few preserves downstairs… but thankfully she had a small jar opened for special occasions and she pulled it from the pantry.

"I have one right here," she whispered.

When the toast was done, she put the slices on plates.

"Allow me," the soldier at the window said, taking the jam from her hands. Opening it, he spooned two generous helpings on each piece, nearly emptying the contents.

Betsy stared in disbelief.

When the coffee was brewed, she poured them each a mug and they began to eat.

"Come join us," the older one offered.

She blindly obeyed.

A lump formed in her throat as she watched them partake, but suddenly some words came to mind. It was a verse her mother had taught her.

"If thine enemy hunger, feed him; if he thirst, give him drink."[7]

"Where's your husband?" the older man asked between bites.

"He's away. Looking for food."

"One of your neighbours said he fixes radios."

Nodding, she clenched her fingers in her lap.

The younger man spoke next. "Your neighbours also say they've seen strange people coming in and out of your home. Is this true?"

Betsy shook her head. *Oh, protect us.*

After they'd eaten, the younger rose and went out back. Betsy watched him go. He made his way to the shop and, on the way back, stopped to talk to the children. What were they telling him?

The man at the table smiled persistently. "Do you have a cellar, Mrs. Vischer?"

Eyes still on the children, Betsy watched the man kneel down in front of Elizabeth and tug gently on her braid. He was being so friendly.

Guard their lips.

"My husband… boarded it up a few years ago." Truth. "We've had problems with mould." Another truth.

She turned to the man. Though he didn't seem satisfied, he didn't ask more. And when the other returned, they got their coats to go.

"You wouldn't mind sending the rest of your bread along with us, would you?" the younger man asked earnestly.

For the first time, Betsy noticed how thin he was.

---

[7] See Romans 12:20.

Her heart pounded. That would've been her family's supper. What would she feed the children? But she couldn't say no. She couldn't take the risk.

Retrieving the loaf, she gave it to him.

I trust you, Lord.

"Thank you for your hospitality." The older man nodded, pulling on his coat. "Please let us know if there's anything we can help you with." He smiled. "And I'm sure your neighbours will keep an eye on things for you. The people of Zeist look out for each other."

And with that, he was gone.

Betsy struggled to breathe. She sat down and her children, having heard the vehicle, rushed inside.

"Mama! Were they actually soldiers?" John asked.

"They were nice," Elizabeth added.

Betsy's heart broke. "Did you tell them anything?"

"No," John assured her.

Henry seemed to be the only one of the three who disliked the fellow. "His breath stank."

"That's enough," she whispered.

She hated them too, but something in her heart made her quiet the boy. It had all felt like too much, and yet God had protected them.

But what about their supper?

Lord, what can I feed my children? Janet's soup kitchen wasn't operating today or else they'd have gone there.

A few minutes passed before she heard a knock at the door.

"Not again," she stammered. But when Elizabeth ran to the window, she squealed, "Aunt Janet!"

John opened the door for her.

"I've brought you something," her sister said with a smile, closing the door behind her and holding out a wooden crate for her inspection.

"What is it?" Betsy asked, having not the strength to rise.

Janet set down the box and pulled out a tulip bulb.

"Planting tulips this fall?" Betsy was confused.

"Perhaps," Janet said. "But that's not what these are for."

Betsy tilted her head. "What then?"

"Soup!"

"Are you joking?"

"Not at all. The idea came to me last night while I was lying in bed."

"Too hungry to sleep?"

Janet waved the question aside. "Add some onion, oil, and a spice if you've got one, and there you have it. Tulip soup. Of course I made sure these didn't have pesticides or chemicals."

"I dug them out of my garden." Amazed, Betsy smiled wearily. "What would Mother think of us eating such a thing?"

"She'd say we're innovative."

"Crazy like always?"

"Exactly."

Betsy couldn't help but smile. It seemed God had provided in record time.

April 1945

The war was over. Canadian soldiers had liberated Holland, and it all felt too good to be true. But Betsy wondered if life would go back to normal. Hank had said they still had a long road ahead of them. The whole country had suffered and it would take years, if not decades, to recover any sort of normalcy.

Life was already looking different. Diederik had gone to live with his niece in Utrecht. His health had greatly declined and he could no longer live alone.

Sem and Eliana would stay with them until they made other arrangements. Sem had found work, and Eliana had an aunt in the next town over with whom she hoped to live. Though it had been hard hiding them away, Betsy would be sorry to see them go. The children too had gotten close with them. But life must go on.

The family sat together in the living room one night. The boys were constructing a tower, Eliana was braiding Elizabeth's hair, Sem hunkered down by the fire reading, and Hank and Betsy sat on the couch.

Hank turned to their sons. "I'll need your help in the shop tomorrow."

Eight-year-old John nodded his agreement, but his younger brother scowled and crossed his arms. "I hate working in the shop," he muttered.

"It doesn't matter," his father quickly replied. "We all need to pitch in to get back on our feet."

"Then I'll get my own job."

Betsy could feel her husband growing tense. Taking his hand, she prayed for patience. The war had worn them thin in more ways than one. Though he was full of the Spirit and faith, Hank Vischer was tired and still struggled not to lose his temper.

"You're too young to get a job, my boy." He shook his head. "And I'm not asking for your help. I'm telling you what needs to be done."

"I'll be leaving first thing tomorrow," Sem cut in. "I'll be staying with a friend until I can find a place to rent."

As she looked at him, Betsy could see he was not well. She hoped he'd be safe.

Draw him to you, she prayed.

Hank nodded. "Be careful, Sem."

Sem shrugged. "I will be."

Eliana spoke next, finished with their daughter's braid. "My aunt is ready to take me on Monday."

"Don't go!" Elizabeth whined, clasping the girl's arms. She'd known Eliana her whole life and they were all fond of her.

"I must, Elizabeth. But I'll write, and I'll come visit as often as I can."

Betsy swallowed her own sadness.

"Life must go on," her husband mused. "Will she be coming for you?"

Eliana nodded.

The fire was dying and Betsy reluctantly slipped from under her afghan and motioned to her daughter.

"Time for bed, Elizabeth," she said.

"It's time for everyone to tuck in," Hank seconded, helping her to her feet. "You boys best be in the shop for eight."

John started heading for their room, but Henry held his ground. "I'm not helping. I was going over to Sven's house tomorrow."

"Did your mother tell you you could?" Hank's voice rose in volume.

"I didn't." Betsy turned to her husband, hoping she could appease the situation. "Could he perhaps help in the afternoon?"

"I'm not helping at all!" The boy kicked his brother's tower, sending it crashing to the ground. Then he stormed from the room.

Her husband moved to follow.

"Let him go," she whispered, and he complied.

The group dispersed and Betsy tucked Elizabeth in. John kissed them goodnight. Hank then guided her towards bed, and she slipped from her baby blue frock and pulled on her nightgown.

He helped her patiently, but his jaw was tense as he eased her into bed.

"I let my temper get the best of me," Hank finally confessed.

"We're all tired."

"I just don't understand that boy."

Smiling, she kissed his palm. "He's passionate and stubborn and fearless… just like his father."

Hank smiled too. "Then *you* must be a patient woman."

Hank presented her with a bouquet of irises the next day. "For my angel."

"Hank!" Betsy smiled from the sofa. Though it was a bright June afternoon, Janet had insisted she build a fire in the hearth. It seemed Betsy just couldn't get warm these days. "Where did you—"

"Mrs. Beekhof was working in her flowerbed this morning when I came by to fix her radio. She didn't have money to pay… but I said the flowers would do."

As she couldn't get outside as much these days, the flowers were a welcome surprise.

Suddenly there was a knock at the door. She felt panic wash over her.

"There now," Hank said soothingly, sitting beside her. "There's nothing to be afraid of."

Feeling foolish, she nodded.

"You put the flowers in water, and I'll get the door."

He helped her from the sofa, and she did as instructed. Of course Hank was right. The war was over and they were safe. But memories were hard to forget. Fear was hard to abandon.

Hands shaking, she trimmed the stems and filled a vase as Hank opened the door. Two men, about the same age as Hank, met him on the other side.

Her husband was quick to invite them inside. "Come in!"

Betsy had never seen these people before, and she wondered who they were.

Hank slapped one on the shoulder. "It's been too long, brother."

"You've become an old man," the visitor replied.

"Look who's talking," the other teased. "You're the bald one."

The three laughed, seeming to forget her presence.

When one of them did catch sight of her, he smiled. "This must be the beauty you don't stop talking about."

"The very one," Hank said, turning to her.

Betsy froze, blushing, as Hank came to her, took the vase, and set it down on the window sill. He ushered her over and smiled.

"This is Betsy, the love of my life."

The two men nodded respectfully.

"But I don't know who you are," she stammered.

Hank took their coats. "These are two of the bravest men I know. May I introduce Gerard Claasen and Luuk van Alphen?"

"You're the brave one, brother," replied Luuk, the younger of the two. He had a friendly smile that made Betsy like him immediately.

"Not brave," Hank said. "Maybe crazy."

The man chuckled. "That too."

Hank invited them to sit and helped her to the couch as well. Sitting beside her, he began to explain. "Reverend Slomp introduced me to these men. We worked together for the resistance, and finer men I've never met."

"You're too generous with your praise," Gerard retorted, shooing away the compliment.

"Hardly," her husband said with a grin.

Gerard turned his attention to Betsy, growing a little more serious. He rolled up his sleeves and stroked his silvery beard. "Has Hank told you of all his brave adventures?"

Betsy swallowed and shook her head. She wanted to know, yet she was afraid of the details. In her opinion, her husband had risked his life too many times. Perhaps it was easier to stay unaware.

But curiosity got the better of her.

"Do tell," she whispered.

"There's not much to tell," Hank remarked.

"I beg to differ," Gerard protested, stroking his beard. "Don't you remember cutting those German lines? Twenty-one wires I think it was…"

Luuk nodded. "I loved watching that pole fall…"

Shivering, Betsy took her husband's hand.

"…oh, I'm sure we could write a book," their bald guest continued to muse.

"Never. I just did my duty, and you did yours." Hank turned to Betsy and swallowed. "And Betsy did hers. She's the real hero. The Gestapo came eight times… eight times!" He turned back to his friends. "And when I had to go underground, she lived on bravely."

"But you were instrumental in distributing information," Gerard said. "Don't brush it off so quickly, my friend."

"Like I said, I just did my duty… fighting for freedom, loving those I was called to love."

The man sighed. "Reverend Slomp always preached love, but it's easier said than done. It's one thing to love the Jews… but what about the Nazis?"

"I don't know if I ever will," her husband replied truthfully.

"I understand, brother." Gerard nodded. "But it's our calling. I spent years learning to forgive my own family, but now I have, and I'm free!"

Hank dropped his gaze and Betsy knew he was thinking of his own father.

"It's not easy," he said.

"I know."

When the two men left, Hank stayed beside her. Though they didn't speak, Betsy's heart swelled with pride.

Her husband was a hero, however much he denied it. He had done what he felt was right and his faith had gotten him through. She stroked his calloused hand, then rested her head on his shoulder. War had been the hardest thing they'd ever gone through. God had answered so many prayers and performed so many miracles, and she was thankful.

But as the previous conversation replayed in her memory, questions arose. Could God work another miracle in their hearts? Could he help Hank forgive those who'd wronged him? Could he help her do the same? She prayed so.

Chapter Twenty-Six

"We're not taking no for an answer, Betsy." Janet was adamant. "We're cleaning your house top to bottom. Spring is here and it must be done."

Betsy watched as her sisters and sister-in-law got to work. The three had rolled up in Janet's Volvo after breakfast and marched in with buckets and rags.

"I am *not* washing baseboards," Hannie declared. "Crawling around on all fours will put a hole in my stockings, to be sure."

Janet threw up her hands. "Then what would you like to do, your highness?" she asked mockingly.

"I'll take the windows," Angela interjected.

"Of course you'll take the windows," Hannie whined. "Everyone knows I clean windows best. I never leave a streak."

Betsy laughed as she took a sip of coffee and watched them from the sofa. The house did need a good cleaning. What would her mother think of all this dust? Betsy simply hadn't had the strength to tackle it herself.

She turned to Hannie. "I happen to know you're good at wiping out cupboards. Your kitchen is always spotless."

Hannie brightened.

"It helps that she has a housekeeper," Angela laughed, slipping on an apron to protect her pretty frock.

Betsy continued. "And Hannie, your kitchen counters are always clear and sparkling."

Her little sister grinned. "I *do* take pride in my kitchen. Though I don't find time to cook very often… I've been so busy with my ladies' committee, you know."

Betsy nodded. Hannie was a social butterfly and thrived on attention. Their father and mother hadn't encouraged flighty behaviour, but they'd been wealthy enough to in some ways make allowance for it. Hannie had gotten new dresses when she wished and attended all sorts of parties. Perhaps their father had been glad to have at least one child who enjoyed being wealthy as much as he had.

The three ladies got to work, happily chatting as they scrubbed.

Betsy visited with them from the couch, resisting the guilt. She should be helping, yet her body wouldn't allow it.

Though she often prayed for a miracle, that the cancer would disappear, she wondered whether God had other plans. Her mother had fought cancer on and off for many years. In the end, she had died… too soon, Betsy had always believed.

She tried not to imagine what might happen to her. The thought of leaving her children without a mother and Hank without a wife made her heart ache.

Hannie sighed, plopping herself down on a dining room chair an hour later. "I think it's about time for lunch."

Janet consulted the clock. "Are you hungry, Betsy?"

"*I'm* hungry!" Hannie piped up. She pushed back a curly wisp.

Betsy laughed. Janet was so very kind to her. Sometimes it seemed she favoured her above the rest.

"I could eat something," Betsy said with a smile.

What she wouldn't give for a sweet *stroopwafel* or a warm *kroket* with mustard. It had been a long time since she'd enjoyed such treats.

Shakily pulling herself from her seat, she set about to prepare something.

"Sit down, Betsy," Janet commanded. "I brought over a potato pie that mustn't go to waste."

Betsy nodded.

Angela grinned. "And I brought a jar of pickled beets left over from last year."

"Sounds appetizing!" Hannie rolled her eyes.

"Stop complaining," Janet reprimanded. "Hannie, you're acting like a schoolgirl."

Their eldest sister washed her hands and pulled the pie from the refrigerator. Getting the oven warming, she found plates and forks in the drawer.

"Speaking of schoolgirls," said Hannie, quickly changing the subject. "Where's Elizabeth? And her brothers for that matter?"

"Elizabeth's gone to a friend's house," Betsy replied, spreading an afghan over her lap.

The Terpstras were some of her children's best friends. They'd even invited Elizabeth to vacation with them multiple times. Though they'd had good intentions, the offer had hurt Hank's pride. *They* had never been able to afford such luxuries. Even before the war, they'd never been able to go on expensive trips.

"Will John and Henry be joining us for lunch?" Janet asked, breaking into Betsy's thoughts while putting the pie in the oven.

"John will," Betsy replied.

She had to admit that she didn't know where Henry was. He'd made such an ordeal about having porridge again for breakfast that he'd stormed away on his bicycle and hadn't been back since. She hadn't had the strength to go after him.

If Hank had been home, he'd never have put up with such behaviour, but he was away too—meeting customers, working tirelessly. Betsy prayed that her son would be home soon. He always came home. But her fear grew nonetheless. Their family seemed to be growing apart. She felt it, and it hurt.

Sustain us, Lord.

When John appeared from his room, the five sat down to eat. Her son looked tired. He had spent the morning and probably most of the night reading. While he loved to get lost in a book, he sometimes paid for it dearly. It seemed to be his way of escape. She and her eldest had always been close, but today even he seemed distant.

Hold us together.

Suddenly the door opened. Was it Henry?

They all turned… but to their surprise, it was their brother.

"Arend, this is a surprise." Betsy tried to stand but couldn't.

As Arend came forward, Angela rose and went to him, taking his hand. "What is it, my love?"

Betsy had never seen him look so distraught. "I wanted to be the first to tell her," he said and turned to Hannie.

Dropping her fork, Hannie rose. "What in the world do you mean?"

"They've taken him." He held her gaze. "They've arrested Isaak."

Janet and Angela were quick to catch their sister's fall.

♪♫♪

"How could they do such a thing?" Betsy turned to her husband that night. "How could they arrest him?"

"He's a traitor, Betsy." Hank was matter-of-fact, unscrewing a small radio by lamplight.

Betsy hated that word. She knew Isaak had helped the Nazis, but he wasn't a villain. Her heart ached for Hannie and the boys. Her sister had come to in hysterics, crying, flailing and demanding to see her husband.

When they'd finally gotten her to settle, Janet had taken her and the boys back to their family home for the night, as Hannie would've refused to be alone, and they all knew it wouldn't be safe. The truth was that she too could be punished.

Hank and Elizabeth had come home around suppertime, and Betsy thanked the Lord that Henry had too. He had arrived just before Hank, so Betsy had put off telling her husband about his behaviour. They'd all had enough difficulty for one day.

Hank now turned to her. "They've arrested Bert Van Aller too."

"What will they do with them?"

Her husband shrugged.

"Will they kill them?"

"I don't know," he answered. "They might just keep them locked up for a while, try and teach them a lesson."

Betsy shivered and wrapped her arms around herself, trying not to imagine such horrors. Her husband stood and took a blanket from the armchair, wrapping it around her shoulders.

"Shall we go to bed?" he asked.

She wouldn't be able to sleep. Though the war was over, the world still felt dark. Her husband was a hero, but Bert and Isaak were behind bars.

Is this justice, Lord? Is this what we've prayed for?

"It still doesn't seem right…" She faltered. "I still don't like it."

For a moment, Betsy saw her husband's jaw clench.

"Would you rather still be invaded?" he asked.

Betsy dropped her head. "Of course not… but neither do I want our friends locked up."

"Can we really call them friends?" Hank's words were sharp. "They betrayed our country and God's people."

Betsy had no more words.

Sighing, Hank sat and took her hand. They were both tired.

🎵

"What's the holdup?" Betsy turned to her sister-in-law. Angela had offered to take her out today. Betsy could no longer comfortably drive, so she didn't get out much at all. Though a homebody, she missed the stores and parks and big blue sky.

Angela had a few things to purchase at the pharmacy, and then they'd go out to lunch.

But traffic was proving slow. They inched along at a snail's pace and could see a crowd gathered ahead.

"Things better hurry up or we'll miss all the good stew!" Angela laughed.

Suddenly, they heard shouting. A few people jumped out of their vehicles and sprinted ahead. Betsy started to feel sick. She'd been nauseous a lot recently, but this was different. She had a bad feeling inside.

"Can we get out?" she asked.

"I don't know…" Angela looked worried. "Are you feeling okay?"

Feeling strangely compelled, Betsy pulled on the door handle.

Go.

Angela killed the engine, as many others were doing, and the two climbed out. Taking Betsy's hand, Angela helped her along. The sound of screaming reached their ears, and Betsy felt goosebumps crawling up her arms.

"Traitor!"

"Take it all off!"

When they reached the crowd, they saw that a circle had formed and someone stood in the middle. A woman. Her stomach churning, Betsy saw a man approach with a set of shears.

"Betsy!" Angela grabbed her arm. "Let's go!"

Betsy shook her head. She had to stay, though she felt as though she'd faint. It was Ada Veenstra, her childhood friend. She'd been stripped of everything but her undergarments, and her hair was next.

Betsy immediately understood. Ada was a traitor. She'd started going out with a German soldier and now she'd pay the price. Others had endured similar fates. Isaak and Bert were being tried. Some had been killed.

Betsy wanted to scream, *Make it stop!* But then, just as quickly, she turned away. Hadn't she felt resentful and bitter towards Ada? Hadn't she herself been angry and unforgiving? After all, Ada had entertained the enemy, the very ones who'd killed Eliana's brother and wreaked havoc on their home. Why should she feel sorry for her?

She looked back. The man with the shears began snipping Ada's beautiful blond locks. They fell in clumps to the ground.

As she watched, Betsy recalled a Bible story her mother had taught her. As she remembered it, a reenactment played out before her eyes. A woman caught in adultery was brought to Jesus. She'd betrayed her family, her husband, and God. "What should we do?" the people had asked Jesus.

What should I do?

Condemnation yelled inside. *She betrayed her country!*

And yet, there was Jesus. Betsy could almost see him now, crouching down, writing in the sand.

Forgive her, Betsy.

But she didn't know if that was possible.

Janet had started to come over almost every day, usually on her own, but sometimes Angela or Hannie tagged along. They were all thankful for Isaak's speedy release, though Bert hadn't been so lucky. Betsy's old admirer was still behind bars and no one knew when or if he'd be let go.

Having come alone today, Janet stood in Betsy's room and waved a brush in the air. "We're tackling your hair, little sister."

Betsy grinned. Her hair *was* a tangled mess, and she had an embarrassing number of split ends. She used to just trim it herself; though she was never as talented as Janet, she'd learned to do simple styles.

But in the last few months, her energy had waned and she felt little strength to do anything. It was hard enough to bathe a few times a week, let alone do any primping.

"If you tilt your head back in the sink, I'll wash you right up," her sister promised, helping Betsy to the bathroom. "Wet hair is best for cutting anyway."

Betsy sat on a chair in front of the sink and leaned back against it, loving the feel of Janet's fingers massaging her scalp and the warmth of the water on her skin. Her sister lathered, rinsed, and towel-dried her hair before they returned to Betsy's room to comb out the strands.

"My goodness, Betsy, your hair looks a sight."

Betsy winced. Seeing herself in the mirror, she swallowed hard. It wasn't just her hair. Her whole appearance had changed, and not for the better. Her skin was turning slightly yellow, jaundice from the cancer spreading to her liver. Her eyes were red, evidence of her lack of sleep. And she was much too thin. Despite everyone's efforts to get her to eat, Betsy had lost her appetite.

She had never been confident in her appearance, but now she was more self-conscious than ever.

"I do look dreadful," she whispered at her reflection.

Janet didn't stop her work. Combing a lock, she held it between two fingers then snipped the bottom few inches.

"You look tired," Janet allowed.

Tears burned and Betsy let them fall.

When Janet looked up, she paused. Crouching down beside her, she wrapped her arms around Betsy's now small frame. Though Janet didn't speak, Betsy was surprised at her sister's tenderness.

"You were always so confident, Janet. Remember when you got me ready for my first date with Hank? I was a basket case, but you've always been so strong."

Her sister sighed and met her gaze. "I was jealous of you, Betsy."

Betsy looked up, surprised by the confession. "Jealous?"

Her sister shrugged, sitting down on the creaky wood floor. "You've always been so sweet—so gentle and pretty."

"I don't feel pretty now." Betsy again eyed her reflection.

Janet met her gaze in the mirror. "You are. You'll just have to believe it."

Betsy giggled like she had when they were girls. "Then you have to believe me as well. You're lovely, Janet—really lovely."

"Lies," her sister mocked, again standing to her feet.

Feeling lighter already, Betsy grinned. "Remember that time Guus Engelhart asked you to the winter gala?"

Her sister chuckled. "It was more of an insult than an invitation. He had asked almost every other girl in school before me."

"He was scared of you."

"As he should've been."

"You refused him on the spot. I remember feeling sorry for the boy. He was so forlorn."

"Why didn't *you* go with him?"

"You wouldn't have let me." Betsy laughed. "Besides, I was far too shy. Neither of us ended up going. What did we do instead?"

"This!" Janet held up her comb. "I did your hair and we blathered all night."

"Much more enjoyable."

"Much more."

Chapter Twenty-Seven

August 1945

"Are you feeling okay today?" John asked, standing by her bed. He held out the warm mug of tea for which she had asked. It seemed she could never quench her thirst, but she tried. Her son had grown tall and was looking more and more grown up every day. He had her fine features and quiet temperament. Her husband said he didn't understand him, but he loved and cared for him well, just like he did for Betsy.

Hank and John spent a lot of time in the shop these days, and Hank spent evenings helping him with his homework. John wanted to attend university one day, but since they couldn't afford tuition he hoped to earn scholarships.

Betsy was so proud of him and prayed for his heart. Like herself, he could grow melancholy. He put so much pressure on himself that sometimes he broke under the weight.

Free him with your love.

Taking the mug, she smiled. "Thank you, my dear." She patted the bed beside her. "Come sit with me."

John obliged and the two sat quietly.

Seeing his serious expression, Betsy touched his chin. "What is it, John?"

"I miss helping you in the garden," he said, his voice cracking.

Betsy's throat tightened. John used to complain about doing that. Though not as vocally as his brother, he'd always said he'd rather study than weed. It was funny the things someone missed… the things one took for granted until they were gone.

"I miss that too," she whispered, taking his hand.

Seeing tears in his eyes, her heart started to break. If only she could take all his pain away. She'd go through any difficulty for her children. What cancer did to their hearts was far worse than what it did to her body.

"We could read together," she offered.

He turned away. "I don't feel like it."

"That's not like you." She touched his shoulders. "I'm still right here, John."

"But what if…" He turned back to her. "What if you die?"

The floodgates opened and he buried his face in her lap.

Betsy took a deep breath, running her hand through his golden blond hair, so like her own.

What am I to say?

♪♫♪

The noise woke her. Her heart pounded before her eyes had even opened. Sharp words spewed from the other room. Henry's voice was loud.

"I don't have to listen to you! You're not my mother!"

"But your mother is sick." Janet's words were firm.

"I hate helping. I hate all of you!"

This time John spoke. "Ever since the war ended, you've been making life terrible for all of us. Don't you think Mother and Father have enough to worry about?"

"I don't care," Henry replied sharply. "They're not around to care either. Father's always gone and Mother's always in bed. And you're not the boss of me!"

"As long as you act like a child, people will treat you like one," Janet reprimanded.

"Frans and Abel don't treat me like a child. They think I'm cool."

Janet snapped back. "You best keep it down, Henry, or you'll wake your mother. Go outside and cool off."

"I don't care. I don't care about any of you. I never asked Father to hide people or help the resistance. I never asked you to come babysit us. If it were up to me, Father would've kept his job at Opa's company and we'd all be rich."

"Like that would've helped," John retorted. "We've just been through a war."

"Uncle Isaak is rich," Henry claimed.

"He also went to university." John's words were prickly. "He didn't drop out and then lie to his parents."

Betsy felt the colour rush to her cheeks. Henry had dropped out of school? Where did he go every day, and why hadn't the school contacted them?

She tried to pull herself up, but her strength failed.

"Henry, go outside," Janet said, raising her voice.

"No! I hate you all, especially you two and the way you try to control my life."

John was getting angry. "You better quit it, Henry! I'll tell Father what you said, and you'll get a whipping."

"Not if I whip you first," his brother threatened.

Betsy heard a chair scrape across the plank floor.

"Boys, stop!" Janet yelled.

The table moved, a chair fell, and the walls rattled. Fists were flying and Henry muttered a curse word.

Betsy couldn't take it. She tried again to rise.

"Stop, stop!" she cried hysterically.

She had to stop them. Clenching the side of her bed, she finally managed to hoist herself up.

But as she attempted to stand, her knees buckled under her. She tried to catch herself on the bedside table but ended up taking that down with her. The lamp fell to the floor and shattered.

Suddenly the door flew open and there were her two sons, wide-eyed and afraid. Janet was on their heels.

"Mother!" John ran to her side.

Betsy had fallen on her right leg and pain coursed through it. Henry stood at a distance, shame written across his face.

"Go call the doctor," Janet commanded him.

Betsy shook her head. "I don't need a doctor, Janet," she whispered.

It was just bruises, she was certain, but it hurt nonetheless.

"I won't take no for an answer." There was a tremble in her sister's voice as she rushed away to make the call herself.

As if it were beckoning, the sun shone brilliantly through her open window.

"Help me outside," she whispered to her boys.

The two gave her their arms and they headed out to the front porch. Her leg boasted a blue bruise, her hip ached from the impact, and her mother's lamp lay in a thousand pieces on the floor inside.

Trying to ignore it all, she studied the boys. John, tall and slender. Henry, muscular and athletic. They sat by her side, worry filling their faces.

"I hate to see you boys fight," she whispered.

John was quick to apologize. "I'm so sorry, Mother."

But Henry remained silent. Remorse shone in his eyes, yet so did the pain that had inspired his behaviour.

Turning to her younger son, she whispered, "I'm sorry, Henry—for losing touch with you."

Almost immediately, her son's tough exterior vanished, and all that was left was a lonely little boy. Her heart ached, and she took both their hands.

"I haven't done everything perfectly. Neither has your father. We've loved you to the best of our ability, but…" Her voice cracked. "…but God's love will last forever. It's strong and dependable."

She turned to John and smiled.

"Because of his love, we don't have to try and be perfect." She then touched Henry's cheek. "Because of his love, we'll never be alone."

"I don't hate you, Mum." Henry's words came quickly.

Understanding what he meant and all that went unsaid, she cupped his face. "I know."

October 1945

Betsy's mouth watered from the delicious smells coming from the kitchen. Today was Hank's birthday and everyone insisted they throw a party.

The whole Baer clan had come over to celebrate. Betsy was thankful that her sisters would tackle the meal.

Her bedroom door sat open and Hank had come to help her to the couch. His beard had flecks of grey. Lines creased his brow, a few wrinkles had formed under his eyes, and he had never looked more handsome.

"Ready to join the party?" he asked with a wink.

Betsy nodded.

He took her in his arms, and Betsy lay her head on his shoulder. Nuzzling his face in her hair, he whispered, "How's my angel?"

"My heart is at rest."

And it was true. Though sadness gripped her heart, though the doctor had said she didn't have long, and though her whole body hurt, she knew God was near.

"I went to see someone today," Hank murmured as they made their way into the living room.

"Who?" Betsy didn't have to wait for a response, for she immediately saw and understood.

Amidst the crowded room full of Baer relatives, Hank's parents and brother sat on the couch. She caught their gaze.

"Hello!" Betsy swallowed. She hadn't seen any of them in months, and Hank had wanted it that way.

Reverend Vischer nodded gravely as usual. "Hello Betsy."

Mrs. Vischer gave her a half-smile, appearing just as confused by the situation as she was. Bram was his usual amiable self, giving Betsy his seat.

Hank sat her down, and she then turned to her husband. Had he really invited his entire family for his birthday? Forgiving the Germans was one thing, but forgiving his family was quite another.

Hank crouched down beside her and smiled. It seemed he didn't feel a need to explain anything.

"Bram has someone he'd like you to meet." Reverend Vischer proudly nodded to Hank.

"Oh?" Hank turned to Bram. His brother was finally finishing seminary, something he'd wanted to do for over a decade. Everyone wondered where he'd take a pulpit. "You back with Fenna?" Hank winked.

Bram shook his head and smiled. "I think I found the one, Hank."

"It's sure taken you long enough," Hank joked.

Bram bristled, and her husband sobered.

"Who's the lucky lady?"

Betsy too was curious, but it was Reverend Vischer who answered. "You remember Reverend de Clerc."

"Your friend from college," Hank said.

His father nodded. "I invited him and his family for a visit a few weeks ago. They did a lot for the resistance, gave almost all they had."

She felt Hank sit a bit straighter. Little did Reverend Vischer know that his own son had done the same.

"They actually hid a Jewish man for over a year," his father went on.

"I see." Hank took Betsy's hand.

"I respect him." The reverend nodded. "I used to speak against such behaviour, but even I can't ignore his bravery."

Betsy wanted to look at her husband, to see if he'd at all betray himself. She resisted the urge.

"Anyway, my friend has a wonderful unmarried daughter…"

"Seems convenient," Hank murmured sarcastically.

This time, Betsy turned to him. Hank could have been bitter, but all she saw was joy. It took everything in her not to shout his praises from the rooftops.

Reverend Vischer, your son is a hero! If you only knew what he did… you'd be proud of him.

But as she studied her husband, she knew she should keep quiet, for though her own heart wanted to hold a grudge, she saw something different in the eyes of the man she loved. Hank Vischer was free. He had experienced the love of God, and now he could eagerly give it away… no matter what he got in return.

♪♩♪

"*I'm* so proud of you." She lay beside her husband that night.

The sun had set early, and everyone had made their way home. The days were getting shorter, and hers were getting fewer. It made her want to savour every moment, including this one.

"I feel like a new man," her husband whispered. "And I want a new start. Go somewhere else."

"Where?" Betsy leaned in closer, pulling the sheet to her chin

"Canada. I've always longed to see it.

Betsy chewed on his words. She'd heard others with similar dreams. Beginning again in a new place, a fresh start, sounded lovely. She didn't know much about Canada, except that for which all Dutch people thanked God: Canada had liberated them from German occupation.

She lay still for a moment, studying Hank's every feature, thanking God that he was still here... that he still had hope for tomorrow. The years had not been easy on him.

He wanted to start over, to feel young again, to give their children new opportunities.

"I think you should do it," she said with a grin.

"*We* should do it," he corrected.

Betsy stroked his cheek, hearing faint birdsong outside. "Hank," she breathed softly. "I won't be with you. We both know that. But I want you to begin again."

Hank was quiet and she knew he was crumbling. She longed to put the pieces back together, but she couldn't. There was more to say, more to arrange, so she prayed he'd be strong.

"After I'm gone, I want you to keep living," she whispered.

"Don't talk like that."

"Promise me you will. Promise me you'll take the children to Canada." Resting her hand on his chest, she let her words linger.

Finally, she felt him give in. "I promise."

December 1945

"I want to braid your hair!" Elizabeth announced, sitting beside her one day. They'd just put up their Christmas tree. The children had, that is. Betsy watched from the sofa, admiring their teamwork.

Hank and the boys had gone out to deliver Christmas cookies and Elizabeth offered to make apple cider on the stove. The two now waited for it to boil.

"You can braid it if you like." Betsy smiled, turning so her daughter could get to work. Currently her daughter wanted to be a hairstylist, and she liked to practice on any willing party.

"Your hair is like a princess's," the girl marvelled.

Betsy did too. She knew very well how thin and brittle her hair had become. But to Elizabeth, it was glorious. Her daughter gently brushed and then braided her locks. When she brought a mirror, Betsy grinned.

"That's the best one yet," she declared.

Laying her head on her shoulder, Elizabeth sighed. "Mama?" she asked after a moment's pause.

"What is it?"

"I'm scared."

"Why?" She ran her fingers through her daughter's wispy curls.

"I'm scared I'm going to forget you."

Unable to speak, Betsy held her daughter even closer. What could she say? Her daughter was young and she might forget a lot of details. *Help, Lord.*

Suddenly, Janet's words came to mind, something she'd told Betsy a long time ago. Betsy hadn't thought of it in years, and she now praised the Lord for such wisdom.

Looking her daughter in the eye, she began slowly. "Elizabeth, you're right. You may forget a lot about me." She didn't want to say it, and her daughter didn't want to hear it, but she would tell her the truth. Summoning her courage, she began again. "You may forget about me, but never forget God."

Wasn't he the one who'd never leave? Wasn't he the one who'd always be there for Hank and the children? His love and presence had gotten her through every trial, and he would take care of her sweet babies too.

The words of the old hymn came back to her, and she slowly began to sing.

The soul that on Jesus doth lean for repose,
I will not, I will not, desert to his foes;
That soul, though all hell should endeavor to shake,
I'll never, no never, no never forsake.

Epilogue

This story is based on the life of my great-grandmother, Elizabeth Visser-Baars. She and her husband Hank helped in the Dutch Resistance during World War II and they had three children together. Betsy went home to be with the Lord after the war and Hank continued on to Canada. Though details have been changed, I've sought to keep the overall story and major plot points historical. May this book remind you that no matter how weak you feel or how dark the night, God is our refuge and strength (Psalm 46:1).

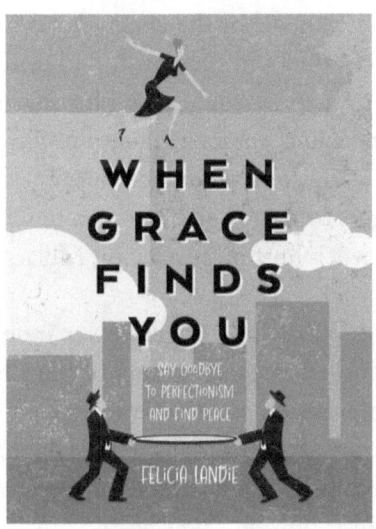

A re you tired of walking the tightrope? Are you trying desperately to be perfect and feel condemned when you fail? Do you struggle to believe that God actually loves you?

I have really good news. You can rest. You can get off the tightrope and know beyond a shadow of a doubt that God loves you.

How? Because God sent his Son to do what we couldn't. He lived, died and rose so that we could be called righteous.

This truth sets us free. Are you ready?

What people are saying about
When Grace Finds You:

This book felt like holding a mirror up to my face. I sure wish I could send a copy back in time to twenty-year-old me; it would have been a relief to know I wasn't alone. Felicia speaks so much truth in these pages—read it and know that you are good in God.

—Michelle Ott, Fellow "Good Girl"

We can easily fall into the lie of the enemy believing that God is hard to please. The truth is: the Lord generously and readily makes his saving grace available to those who would seek him through his Son. Felicia provides a well-articulated testimonial of wrestling with the Lord in Scripture over this truth. Join her on her journey of tasting the grace of the Lord who delights to readily give it to you in Christ Jesus.

—Rev. Travis Johnston, Instructor, Millar College of the Bible

With all tact and humility, Felicia gives us a fresh look into perhaps the most foundational-yet-forgotten tenet of the Christian faith: grace. Sharing from experiences oh so familiar to any believer, Felicia speaks Biblical truth to soothe, steady, and inspire the doubting and jaded soul. *Tasting Grace* is a beautiful reminder I'll be keeping on the nightstand where I can reach for it time and time again.

—Karis Turner, Wife, Mother, and "Grace Person" in training

This book provides a fresh look at how God relates to us, especially in the difficult personal journeys that most of us will face at one time or another. Its many stories and illustrations will keep you turning the pages. Some will make you laugh, others may bring tears, but either way, they will make you think and rethink your understanding of God's unconditional love for us all.

—Paul Chamberlain, PhD., Professor of ethics, apologetics and leadership, Trinity Western University

As a child I was taught to say grace before a meal. We couldn't wait until grace was finished so we could eat. Felicia reminds us not to move on past grace to the meal but to taste grace. Grace is sweet. Grace is satisfying. Grace is greater than all my sins.

—Kelvin Thiessen, Director of Admissions at Millar College of the Bible